## *FROM THE NANCY DREW FILES*

*THE CASE:* *Nancy investigates a piano competition that has turned fierce . . . and potentially fatal.*

*CONTACT:* *Ted Martinelli seems to believe that he and Nancy could play some beautiful music together.*

*SUSPECTS:* Maura MacDonald—*A semifinalist, she stands to move into the finals if one of the top competitors should meet with an accident.*

Alexander Poliakin—*One of the three finalists, he is driven by ambition and an absolute will to win.*

Grace Hammel—*A last-minute replacement on the judges' panel, she may have a personal stake in the competition's outcome.*

*COMPLICATIONS:* *Nancy is used to facing risks, but the emotions stirred in her by Ted Martinelli could be the most dangerous of all.*

**Books in The Nancy Drew Files® Series**

#1 SECRETS CAN KILL
#2 DEADLY INTENT
#3 MURDER ON ICE
#4 SMILE AND SAY MURDER
#5 HIT AND RUN HOLIDAY
#6 WHITE WATER TERROR
#7 DEADLY DOUBLES
#8 TWO POINTS TO MURDER
#9 FALSE MOVES
#10 BURIED SECRETS
#11 HEART OF DANGER
#16 NEVER SAY DIE
#17 STAY TUNED FOR DANGER
#19 SISTERS IN CRIME
#31 TROUBLE IN TAHITI
#35 BAD MEDICINE
#36 OVER THE EDGE
#37 LAST DANCE
#41 SOMETHING TO HIDE
#43 FALSE IMPRESSIONS
#45 OUT OF BOUNDS
#46 WIN, PLACE OR DIE
#49 PORTRAIT IN CRIME
#50 DEEP SECRETS
#51 A MODEL CRIME
#53 TRAIL OF LIES
#54 COLD AS ICE
#55 DON'T LOOK TWICE
#56 MAKE NO MISTAKE
#57 INTO THIN AIR
#58 HOT PURSUIT
#59 HIGH RISK
#60 POISON PEN
#61 SWEET REVENGE
#62 EASY MARKS
#63 MIXED SIGNALS
#64 THE WRONG TRACK
#65 FINAL NOTES
#66 TALL, DARK AND DEADLY
#68 CROSSCURRENTS
#70 CUTTING EDGE
#71 HOT TRACKS
#72 SWISS SECRETS
#73 RENDEZVOUS IN ROME
#74 GREEK ODYSSEY
#75 A TALENT FOR MURDER
#76 THE PERFECT PLOT
#77 DANGER ON PARADE
#78 UPDATE ON CRIME
#79 NO LAUGHING MATTER
#80 POWER OF SUGGESTION
#81 MAKING WAVES
#82 DANGEROUS RELATIONS
#83 DIAMOND DECEIT
#84 CHOOSING SIDES
#85 SEA OF SUSPICION
#86 LET'S TALK TERROR
#87 MOVING TARGET
#88 FALSE PRETENSES
#89 DESIGNS IN CRIME
#90 STAGE FRIGHT
#91 IF LOOKS COULD KILL
#92 MY DEADLY VALENTINE
#93 HOTLINE TO DANGER
#94 ILLUSIONS OF EVIL
#95 AN INSTINCT FOR TROUBLE
#96 THE RUNAWAY BRIDE
#97 SQUEEZE PLAY
#98 ISLAND OF SECRETS
#99 THE CHEATING HEART
#100 DANCE TILL YOU DIE
#101 THE PICTURE OF GUILT
#102 COUNTERFEIT CHRISTMAS
#103 HEART OF ICE
#104 KISS AND TELL
#105 STOLEN AFFECTIONS
#106 FLYING TOO HIGH
#107 ANYTHING FOR LOVE
#108 CAPTIVE HEART
#109 LOVE NOTES

Available from ARCHWAY Paperbacks

# The NANCY DREW Files™ 109

# LOVE NOTES

CAROLYN KEENE

AN ARCHWAY PAPERBACK
Published by POCKET BOOKS
New York London Toronto Sydney Tokyo Singapore

This book is a work of fiction. Names, characters, places and incidents are products of the author's imagination or are used fictitiously. Any resemblance to actual events or locales or persons, living or dead, is entirely coincidental.

AN ARCHWAY PAPERBACK *Original*

An Archway Paperback published by
POCKET BOOKS, a division of Simon & Schuster Inc.
1230 Avenue of the Americas, New York, NY 10020


Produced by Mega-Books, Inc.



ISBN: 0-671-88200-7

First Archway Paperback printing July 1995

10 9 8 7 6 5 4 3 2 1



Cover art by Cliff Miller

Printed in the U.S.A.

IL 6+

# LOVE NOTES

# Chapter One

"WHAT A PERFECT DAY!" Bess Marvin exclaimed, pulling off her baseball cap and smiling at her friend Nancy Drew. "I love feeling the wind in my hair."

"Even if all that gorgeous hair gets messed up?" Nancy teased.

"Joke all you want, Nan, but I know you're glad I talked you into renting this convertible," Bess said.

Nancy was really enjoying the drive up the winding mountain road, and she had to admit a convertible made it even more exciting. As the car reached the summit, Nancy stopped so they could look down into the valley. The morning sun was glistening on the dewy grass and red barns poked up here and there.

"This view should be on a postcard," Bess said as she snapped a picture with her camera.

Nancy smiled. "Dad was right. This is the perfect place for a vacation." She grinned mischievously. "Not much chance of anything mysterious happening around all those cows," she added, pointing.

Bess laughed. "You never know what we might find at the music festival—other than cute musicians, I mean."

Nancy Drew's father, lawyer Carson Drew, had suggested that Nancy spend a couple of weeks in late July with an old friend of his, Mrs. Myrna Wheeler. She lived in the small town of Westbridge, known for the Muscatonic Summer Music Festival.

Nancy had jumped at the chance to visit the beautiful town, nestled in the heart of the Berkshire Mountains, in western Massachusetts. She and Bess had flown to Boston on Thursday, the afternoon before, rented a car, then drove two hours to Westbridge. They spent the evening with Mrs. Wheeler.

She filled them in on the outdoor symphony concert schedule at the festival and the world-famous piano competition that was taking place that week. Three finalists had been selected, Mrs. Wheeler explained. Their final performances were scheduled for Monday.

Until then Nancy and Bess decided to explore the surrounding towns, attend one outdoor concert, and relax.

"I'm just sorry George can't see this," Bess said, pointing to a sparkling stream bordered by gold and purple wildflowers that they passed beside the road.

"I hope that course she signed up for is fun," Nancy said. George Fayne, Bess's cousin and Nancy's close friend, had decided to spend the summer studying stage management at the local theater in their hometown, River Heights.

The steep mountain road finally leveled off when they reached the valley floor.

"Well, where to?" Nancy asked.

Bess opened the glove compartment and took out a map.

"We have the whole morning and part of the afternoon to explore before the concert later," Nancy went on.

"Slow down!" Bess shouted. "I just saw a sign for horses and riding trails."

"That sounds like fun," Nancy said. She turned at the next intersection and headed back toward the sign Bess had seen. As they pulled up to a tall wooden gate, Bess read, " 'Chapin's Horse Farm. Training and Boarding. Forest trails. Inquire within.' I think we'd be able to ride here, don't you?" Bess's blue eyes sparkled.

"Let's give it a try," Nancy said. She pulled the car into the driveway and headed for the barn.

Nancy chose a black gelding named Allegro for herself and a gentle gray mare named Andante for Bess. As the groom saddled them up and helped them mount the horses, Bess giggled nervously.

"I hope I can do this," she said. The groom led them out of the paddock and pointed out one of the farm's many trails. He explained that it circled around the nearby woods and pastures and led back to the stables.

Nancy smiled and stroked her horse's neck. "Don't worry, Bess. Your horse looks nice and gentle. Anyway, her name is a good sign."

"Why? What does it mean?" Bess asked, tightening her grip on the reins.

"*Andante* means 'slow' in Italian. It's also used as a music term. I learned it in music appreciation," Nancy said. "I guess everyone around here is affected by the music festival in one way or another."

"So what does *allegro* mean?" Bess asked, following Nancy as they started along the trail.

"It means 'fast'!" Nancy laughed as Allegro trotted ahead, eager to canter down the trail.

Nancy reined him in and waited for Bess to catch up. With her shoulder-length reddish blond hair, sparkling blue eyes, and slender build, Nancy and her horse could have posed in an ad for Massachusetts tourism.

Keeping their horses to a walk, the girls rode along the forest trail, ducking to avoid occasional branches. Sunlight streamed down through the gaps in the dense pine forest, and the smell of warm pine needles on the forest floor was inviting. Soon Bess began to relax and enjoy the ride.

As they rounded a curve in the path, they spotted two horses ahead of them.

The trail widened as they caught up to the horses, and there was enough room to stop and chat. One of the riders was a very handsome guy, Nancy noticed. She figured he was around twenty. He had blond hair, sparkling green eyes, and an athletic build, and seemed very comfortable on horseback. He was wearing cutoffs and a dark green T-shirt. The other rider was a girl who Nancy thought looked about seventeen or eighteen, with waist-length glossy black hair. She was wearing jeans and a white, long-sleeved blouse. She seemed less at ease.

"Hi, I'm Nancy Drew, and this is Bess Marvin," Nancy said, smiling warmly.

Bess's smile was less confident. She seemed

flustered as her horse danced nervously around the other horses.

The young man reached over and calmed Bess's horse by speaking quietly to it and stroking its neck. "Don't worry," he said to Bess. "She just doesn't like to feel crowded. I rode her yesterday. She's fine." He smiled at Bess and Nancy and said, "I'm Ted Martinelli. This is Keiko Yamamoto."

The girl smiled shyly at them. Nancy smiled in return, then spoke to Ted. "I'm impressed with the way you calmed Andante. You have a real feel for horses. Do you work with them?"

Ted laughed. "Not exactly," he said. "I'm a musician."

"Oh, are you here for the festival?" Nancy asked.

"Yes," Ted answered. "Keiko and I are both in the piano competition."

"Oh!" Bess responded, her eyes lighting up. "How exciting!"

Ted smiled. "Yes, what you have here are two-thirds of the Muscatonic Piano Competition finalists."

Keiko added, "The third finalist doesn't ride, or he would have come with us. This is our morning to relax."

"Don't you have to practice for several hours every day?" Nancy asked.

Keiko and Ted both nodded. "Our practice schedule at the festival has been ferocious—we've had to get up very early in order to fit in the required hours," said Keiko. She grinned and glanced at Ted. "Ted doesn't mind so much," she continued, "because he's a morning person. But I'm a night owl, and I have trouble getting up."

"How long do you practice every day? Do you enter other contests? Do you get to travel a lot?" Bess's questions came out in a rush. She was clearly fascinated with the idea that these two could be world-famous pianists.

Ted laughed. "Whoa, one question at a time!" Turning to Keiko, he said, "Why don't you tell them about the contest circuit, and then I'll tackle the question about our practice routine."

His horse, a black-and-white Appaloosa, whinnied, impatient to be on the move again. Ted tightened his hold on the reins. "Why don't we keep riding as we talk?" he suggested. "My horse is starting to get restless."

As the trail curved and narrowed, Nancy and Ted took the lead and Bess and Keiko followed. Riding, Keiko described the routine followed by most concert pianists their age. They entered all the major world-class competitions and competed against one another month after month, sometimes year after year. This routine ended when a pianist finally won a major prize or gave up the dream of pursuing a solo career.

"Is it important to win a major contest? Can you have a career without a first prize?" Nancy asked.

"Sometimes it happens, if you're very lucky, but usually you cannot make it without winning at least one contest," Keiko said.

"There are so many good pianists these days," Ted explained, "that if you don't have something that makes you stand out, it's hard to get concert bookings or a record contract."

"Isn't it scary, playing in front of judges all the time?" Bess asked.

"No, you get used to it," Ted said. "Musicians who can't handle stress don't get very far."

Nancy nodded sympathetically. "It's sort of like being an actor, isn't it?" she asked. "You may get stage fright just before you go on, but it disappears the minute you say your first line—or play the first note, in your case."

"That's it exactly," Ted said, grinning at Nancy. She noticed that his eyes crinkled at the corners when he smiled.

"How old were you when you started playing?" Bess asked Keiko.

"I was three," Keiko replied. She smiled at Bess's surprised expression. "They start us early in Japan."

"I, on the other hand, didn't start until the ripe old age of seven," Ted said, laughing. "Keiko was already playing on TV shows when she was that age—she was a real child prodigy," he explained. "When I was little I did practice several hours a day because I loved it so much. But I'm not so disciplined now," he added, grinning. "A couple of years ago I discovered windsurfing. Growing up in California, it's amazing that it took me so long!"

"And somewhere along the way, you also learned to ride pretty well," Nancy said with a smile.

"Yeah, well, I guess you could say I'm a frustrated athlete." Ted smiled self-consciously and patted his horse's sleek neck.

This guy is multitalented, Nancy thought. And he seems so modest. She wondered if there was anything he couldn't do. She watched him guide his horse easily along the forest trail as it started down a hill and narrowed.

"Who is the third finalist?" Bess asked.

"His name is Alexander Poliakin. He's from Russia," Keiko said. Just then the path narrowed even more and the horses jostled to accommodate one another. Ted took the lead, followed by Bess and then Nancy, with Keiko bringing up the rear.

Two minutes later a scream shattered the peace of the forest. Nancy was shocked as Keiko's horse galloped past her down the hill, the empty saddle askew. Nancy quickly turned and saw Keiko lying motionless on the ground!

# Chapter Two

NANCY SHOUTED to alert the others, then jumped off her horse and ran to help Keiko. After checking the girl's pulse, Nancy gently chafed her wrists, hoping to wake her. After a few moments Keiko's lids fluttered and she moaned.

"Easy, Keiko, you've had a bad fall," Nancy said gently. Ted and Bess had dismounted and were looking on with concern.

"What—I mean, how did I . . ." Keiko seemed disoriented, and Nancy quickly tried to reassure her.

"Your horse bolted for some reason, and your saddle became loose. It's probably a good thing that you fell free of the horse. Are you hurt anywhere? Can you move your legs and arms?"

Gingerly, Keiko moved each leg and lifted her arms. When she tried to rotate her right wrist, she winced with pain.

"Oh, no!" Ted exclaimed softly. He bent down and very gently took Keiko's right hand in his own. Turning to Nancy, he said urgently, "We must get her to a doctor immediately. This could be a serious injury."

He stood up and remounted his horse. "I'll ride back to the stables and try to get hold of the festival doctor," he said. "I'm sure he'll come out here if I tell him what happened."

Nancy nodded. "Good idea," she said.

Bess knelt beside Nancy and smiled sympathetically at Keiko. "Don't worry," she said. "I'll bet it's nothing very serious. I once sprained my wrist in a skiing accident, and it was back to normal within a few days."

"A few days?" Keiko said with a groan. She looked at her bruised wrist fearfully. "The final performance is on Monday, and I've got to practice. I don't believe this is happening," she said.

"Do you think you can get up?" Nancy asked gently. "You'd probably be more comfortable back at the stables."

Keiko nodded, then got to her feet shakily, leaning on Bess and Nancy for support. Suddenly she said, "There was something wrong with that saddle. It didn't just come loose when I fell. I could feel it loosen as I rode."

Nancy and Bess made eye contact above Keiko's head, and Nancy came to a quick decision. "Keiko, I'm going to find your horse and bring him back. Bess, will you help Keiko back to the stables? You can ride double on Andante."

Bess nodded. "Of course, Nan." She put her arm reassuringly around Keiko's shoulder.

"I think we should try to find out what caused the horse to bolt like that," Nancy said as she helped Keiko into the saddle and gave Bess a boost so she could sit behind the pianist. She paused, smiling at the distraught Keiko. "Don't worry. I'm sure Ted will get the doctor."

Keiko nodded distractedly, and Nancy watched as she and Bess started back up the trail to the stables. Bess took off her blue cardigan and wrapped it loosely around Keiko's shoulders. Nancy could hear her talking soothingly to Keiko as they moved away.

Quickly Nancy remounted her horse and rode off down the path in the opposite direction. She held Allegro to a walk, although the horse strained against the reins, sensing that something was wrong.

As she rode, Nancy peered carefully through

the dense foliage on either side of the trail, trying to spot the runaway horse. What could have spooked the gentle gelding like that? Nancy wondered. They had been riding along peacefully. There had been no sudden movement that Nancy could remember, and no loud noise.

Since Keiko had been the last in line, something could have happened behind her that the rest of the group was unaware of. Nancy searched her memory, playing the scene over again in her head.

Suddenly she saw someone approaching on horseback. As the horse drew nearer, Nancy could see that it was a mare with a white star on its forehead.

The rider was a middle-aged man. He sat very tall in the saddle. As he approached, he raised his hand in greeting.

"Hi!" he said in a friendly tone.

"Hello," Nancy replied. The man's face was very familiar, and for a moment Nancy found herself staring at him, trying to remember where she had seen him before.

Suddenly it came to her: the cleft chin, the sharply chiseled features, the thick shock of silver hair—this man had to be Curt Lucas, the award-winning Broadway composer.

Nancy had seen him many times on television, receiving awards or being interviewed about his musicals. And earlier that morning she had seen his picture in the brochure for the music festival. He was one of the judges of the piano competition.

Curt Lucas smiled at Nancy. She blushed, realizing that her thought process must have been pretty clear to him. Oh well, he must be used to it, Nancy thought. Although his face wasn't as famous as that of a rock star or a movie star, it was still a well-known face.

"Sorry, I didn't mean to stare," Nancy said. "It's just that—of course—I recognized you."

"That's all right, think nothing of it," Lucas said graciously. "But now you have the better of me—you obviously know who I am, but I don't know who you are."

"I'm Nancy Drew." Nancy smiled as the composer maneuvered his horse close enough to reach over and shake her hand. Nancy noticed that the horse Lucas was riding was a beautiful animal, with a dark shiny coat and large liquid eyes.

"I don't suppose you're looking for a runaway horse," Lucas said.

"Yes!" Nancy replied excitedly. "Have you seen him—a large chestnut gelding?"

"Yes, as a matter of fact I have. I passed him grazing peacefully in the field just over that hill." He chuckled. "But he couldn't fool me. I knew he was a runaway—the saddle was still attached." He added, "I hope the rider's okay."

"I'm not sure," Nancy said. "As a matter of fact, you must know her—the pianist Keiko Yamamoto—and I think her right hand has been injured."

"What?" Lucas shouted. "Where is she now?"

"She's heading back to the stables. She was riding with Ted Martinelli. He rode ahead to call the festival doctor."

"I'd better go see her. Maybe there's something I can do." The composer started to ride off. "I hope this doesn't mean she can't play," he said. "What a thing to happen!"

Nancy rode toward the meadow Lucas had mentioned. As she came over the rise, she could see Keiko's horse, just as Lucas had described him, grazing peacefully. She rode slowly up to the gelding, anxious not to spook him again, but he barely seemed interested in her approach. He just flared his nostrils and whinnied softly.

Slowly Nancy dismounted and moved closer to the great horse. She patted his neck and talked gently to him.

"Hello, boy. Are you feeling calmer now?" she asked. As she straightened the loose saddle and started to tighten the leather girth, she noticed that the strap seemed to be broken.

She looked at it closely, then drew her breath in sharply. It had been cut almost completely through on the underside. The cut didn't show on the top of the strap, so anyone adjusting it wouldn't notice. The strap would pull apart slowly as the ride went on.

Nancy tightened the saddle as best she could with the broken girth, while the horse whinnied nervously and pawed the ground. Nancy stroked him gently. "Don't worry, boy, I'm not going to hurt you," she began, but as the horse continued to whinny, it occurred to her that perhaps the saddle was irritating him.

Nancy lifted the saddle up a few inches and took a closer look at the horse's side. On his flank, just at the point where a rider puts pressure with the knees, Nancy found a large burr digging into the tender skin. There was no doubt about it: someone had deliberately sabotaged Keiko's horse!

# Chapter Three

GENTLY Nancy removed the burr from the horse's side. She held it up and examined it. It was large and round with needle-sharp spines. No wonder the horse threw Keiko and took off, she thought grimly. Whoever did this meant business.

After putting the burr in her pocket, Nancy quickly remounted Allegro. She led Keiko's horse back to the stable, then headed for the tack room and office with the saddle. She found Ted, Keiko, and Bess there, waiting for the festival doctor.

Nancy put the heavy saddle down on the owner's desk and showed him how the girth had been weakened by slicing it halfway through. Bess and Ted watched as Mr. Chapin examined the strap with a confused expression on his face. Finally he looked up and said, "I don't understand this. No one who works for me would have done this. I trust them all implicitly."

Nancy removed the burr from her pocket. "I'm not accusing your employees, Mr. Chapin," she said, "but someone sliced that girth and then deliberately placed this burr under the horse's saddle."

"Can I see that?" Ted asked Nancy. He examined it carefully, turning it around and around in his hands. "I don't know about pine forests in this part of the country," he said grimly, "but if they're anything like pine forests back home, this burr could not have come from around here."

Mr. Chapin nodded. "You're right. That's a burr from a horse chestnut, and there aren't any on my property that I know of." He paused, then added with a worried frown, "I'm going to round up the stablehands to see if they know anything about this." As he left the office, he asked Nancy to let him know when the doctor arrived.

"Do you mean someone deliberately brought this burr here?" Bess asked. "Why would they do that?"

Instead of answering, Ted glanced at Keiko, who sat quietly on a chair in the corner of the office. Bess's sweater was now wrapped around Keiko's hand.

Keiko got up and joined the others. "Let me see the saddle," she said. She looked at the stretched-out strap with disbelief, then examined the burr.

"It seems that someone really wanted me to have an accident," Keiko said, her voice very low.

"It does look pretty bad," Ted said, putting an arm around her. "But maybe we can find out who's responsible."

Keiko hesitated, then gazed shyly at Nancy. "Bess told me about your experience as a private investigator," she said slowly. "Do you think you could check into this?"

"That's a good idea," Ted said. "Would you? Not just for Keiko, but for all of us. For all we know, someone might be out to sabotage us all."

"I'd be happy to help," Nancy said.

Keiko acted relieved. "Thank you," she said gratefully. "I feel much better knowing we have you on our side."

Ted smiled at Nancy. "So do I," he said warmly. "We might be able to find you and Bess a room at our dorm," he suggested, "so you could be closer to the festival." Their eyes met, and Nancy felt a charge pass between them, like a small electric shock. Hold it, she warned herself. Since when do you respond to anyone other than Ned Nickerson? She decided to keep a tight rein on her emotional response to this guy.

"By the way," Nancy asked Keiko, "did Curt Lucas find you? I met him when I was looking for your horse, and he was extremely concerned about your hand."

"Yes, he was here," Keiko replied. "He made a generous offer to help in any way he could."

"We told him the doctor was on his way and there wasn't much he could do by hanging around. He had to leave for a judges' meeting," Ted added.

"I can't believe that was *the* Curt Lucas!" Bess said excitedly. "We've only been here one day, and so far we've met two fabulous pianists and one of the most famous composers in the world!"

"I'd wait till you hear us play before you call us fabulous," Ted said with a grin.

The office door swung open and a man entered, carrying a black bag. He had snowy white hair and wire-rimmed glasses. He looked so much like a storybook country doctor that Nancy almost giggled. "Are you the festival doctor?" she asked.

"Yes, I'm Dr. Frankel. Who's the girl with the injury? Ah, it must be you," he said, spotting Keiko's hand wrapped in the blue sweater. He smiled kindly. "Let's have a look at that."

As he carefully unwrapped the sweater and started his examination, Nancy quietly left to talk to Mr. Chapin. He was in the stable with two frightened-looking teenage boys.

"Mr. Chapin, the doctor has arrived," Nancy called from the doorway. Mr. Chapin turned and gestured for her to come in.

"Ms. Drew, I'd like you to meet Dan and Robby Gallagher. I've been teaching them to look after the horses."

Nancy smiled and said hello.

"I've been asking them what they know about Tristan's saddle," Mr. Chapin continued.

"We don't know how that accident could've happened, honest, Mr. Chapin," Robby said.

"We weren't actually here when those two came in and saddled up," Dan added.

"What do you mean, you weren't here?" Mr. Chapin demanded. "I thought you said everything was normal and there were no problems?"

"Well, there weren't any problems," Robby rushed to explain. "We laid out the saddles, brought out the horses, and then there was something we had to do, so we left, just for a few minutes."

"What on earth was so important that you had to leave for a few minutes?" Mr. Chapin shouted.

"Well, it's just that—" Robby shot a guilty look at his brother, then continued bravely, "it's just that they were interviewing the new Red Sox pitcher on the radio, and it was exactly at ten o'clock, and we just had to hear it," he finally said in a rush.

"Well, why didn't you say so to begin with!" Mr. Chapin thundered, thoroughly exasperated. "You see how it was, Ms. Drew," he added, turning to Nancy.

"Yes, I do see," Nancy said. Turning to the boys, she added, "So you didn't help Keiko and Ted saddle up. Did you actually see them arrive?"

"Well, no," Robby said. "But we knew they were coming around ten, and when they weren't here on the dot, we thought they'd probably be late. So we just ran for the office so we could hear the—"

"Yes, all right, boys, I think that's enough," Mr. Chapin said, leading Nancy from the barn. Nancy smiled at the two boys as she left, thinking that she would have liked to ask just a few more questions. She decided she'd try to come back later.

"You see?" Mr. Chapin repeated. "The only schemes those two would cook up would have to do with baseball."

"Yes," Nancy said thoughtfully, "I see your point. But I do wonder who else could have had access to the stable before Ted and Keiko arrived. And who else might have known they were coming?"

"Well, I can answer that one," Mr. Chapin said. "I post the rental schedule on the board outside the stable, so anyone could have seen the names there. And as for who else had access, well, the stable isn't locked. I suppose, since no one seems to have been around at the time, anyone could have gone in and done the damage." He sighed. "I guess this means I'd better pay more attention to security around here."

As they entered the office, Nancy was glad to see that the atmosphere inside was calm. Keiko's wrist was wrapped in a secure-looking white bandage, and she was actually smiling.

"Oh, Nan, she's going to be all right!" Bess said.

"Yes," Dr. Frankel added. "This young lady has been very fortunate. It's only a very minor sprain with localized bruising. If she keeps her wrist stable, she should be able to practice later today with almost no pain at all."

"Thank you so much—you are a genius!" Keiko said.

"Nothing of the sort—you were just lucky," Dr. Frankel said. He handed her a tiny bottle containing two white pills. "Don't forget, if there's severe pain, take one of these pills. Just one. It may make you sleepy, but it will relieve the pain. You can take another tomorrow if you need it." He rolled down his sleeves, and picked up his black bag. "Well, I'm off. Call me again if you need me."

After the doctor left, Nancy and Bess offered Ted and Keiko a lift back to the festival grounds. Ted declined, explaining that he had a motorcycle parked outside, but Keiko accepted gratefully.

"I don't blame you a bit, Keiko," Ted said. "You'll be better off in a car than riding on the back of my bike." Then he added, "Why don't we all meet at the early afternoon concert?" He glanced at his watch. "It's just about noon now, and the concert starts at twelve forty-five on the Great Lawn. We can pick up some food and have a picnic lunch. How about it?"

"Sounds good to me," Nancy said.

Bess agreed enthusiastically. "Are you up for it, Keiko?"

"Definitely!" the pianist replied. "Now that I know my wrist isn't badly hurt, I feel terrific. Bring on the Beethoven!"

"Why don't you girls follow me back to the festival," Ted suggested. "I know a shortcut, and we'll avoid traffic on the main road."

He got on his bike and adjusted his helmet, then took off with a small explosion of dust and gravel. Nancy followed him toward the main road, with Keiko in the front seat and Bess in the back.

Bess sighed. "Isn't he the most romantic guy you ever met?" she asked Nancy.

"He's definitely interesting," Nancy replied, her tone carefully neutral.

"He's a very good pianist," Keiko added earnestly. The three girls burst out laughing.

Nancy pulled into the festival parking lot behind Ted and parked the car. Together they headed for the Great Lawn, where the concert would take place.

"It's such a good spot to hear music," Ted said, ushering them into the food tent to pick up picnic lunches.

"Doesn't the sound sort of evaporate when it's played outside?" Bess asked.

"It probably would, but the orchestra plays inside a building that's completely open on one side. It looks sort of like a shell. See, there it is." Ted pointed across the lawn.

"It's got about six thousand seats inside, but the sound is just as good on the lawn, where people can sit on blankets and have picnics. At night you can listen to the music and lie down watching the stars. It's very romantic," he said, letting his gaze rest on Nancy for a moment.

They each chose a sandwich and strawberries with fresh cream. Then, carrying their lunches, they searched for the perfect spot on the lawn.

It was beginning to fill up, but Ted spotted a good place under an oak tree.

"This is so exciting!" Bess said. Some of the musicians had emerged from behind the shell and were starting to tune up. Ted had managed to borrow a plaid blanket from the festival office, and he opened it up and spread it on the ground under the tree.

"I love listening to music outside like this," Nancy said. "It's so different. More . . ." she stopped, at a loss for words.

"More powerful, perhaps?" asked a voice with an exotic accent.

They all turned to see a young man with long dark hair and a dark beard, carrying a large picnic basket. He had broad shoulders and stooped posture. He was almost bearlike as he settled near them on the lawn.

"Alexander!" Keiko exclaimed. "He is our missing third finalist," she explained to Nancy and Bess, introducing them. Then turning back to Alexander, she asked, "Did you have a good morning?" Without waiting for a response, she held up her injured hand. "It's a good thing you didn't come riding with us after all. Look what happened to me."

Nancy was relieved to see that Keiko was smiling as she said this. She seemed to have gotten over the shock of the accident.

Alexander stared at Keiko's hand. "What happened?" he asked, taking in both Keiko and Ted.

Ted shrugged. "Keiko's horse decided to make a run for it," he said casually. He caught Nancy's eye, and she understood that he wanted to play down the importance of the incident for the time being.

"Are you going to be able to play?" Alexander asked, his voice tense. "We've got rehearsals with the orchestra today, you know. The concerto rehearsals."

"I've had my rehearsal switched to tomorrow, although the doctor thinks I'll be fine by this evening." She laughed. "And I feel fine already."

Shyly, Alexander offered to share some of

his lunch, a special mushroom salad he had prepared himself.

"I picked the mushrooms in the woods this morning," he said. "If you've never had a mushroom salad, you should really try it—it's a Russian specialty. I am from Russia. In all Russian homes, guests are offered a meal of wild mushrooms to make them feel welcome."

Nancy declined, explaining that she already had more food than she could possibly finish. Bess agreed, and Keiko and Ted both explained they didn't really like mushrooms. Alexander frowned, shrugged, and started eating his salad.

Just as they were finishing their lunch, music filled the air. Ted leaned close to Nancy and whispered that it was Beethoven's Fifth Symphony. Nancy relaxed and let the music wash over her. It was a glorious feeling to be outside on a perfect day listening to one of the most famous pieces of music ever written.

Without warning Nancy heard harsh coughing behind her. She turned just in time to see Alexander collapse, his face bright red!

# Chapter Four

"Is there a doctor here?" Nancy shouted as she quickly bent over Alexander and loosened his collar. She felt helpless as the pianist continued to cough. He wasn't choking on food, or she would have used the Heimlich maneuver. Something else was wrong.

Bess, Ted, and Keiko all offered suggestions, but no one really knew what to do. Bess tried to cushion Alexander's head, but he was coughing so badly that it didn't seem to help. An employee approached holding a cellular phone, and asked if she could help.

"Yes! Please call an ambulance, fast!" Nancy said. She watched anxiously as Alexander's face turned a deeper shade of red and his coughing worsened. He gasped for air, unable to catch his breath.

Checking for any clue as to what could have caused this severe a reaction, Nancy noticed Alexander's picnic basket lying open on the blanket. She pawed through it for anything that might be responsible for his condition. There was a plastic container half-full of the marinated wild mushroom salad and a hard roll filled with cheese and tomatoes. She put these items in her shoulder bag.

"Do you think it was something in his food?" Bess asked.

"Could be," Nancy said. "What else would have caused such a bad reaction?" She took hold of Alexander's hand as he continued to cough and toss helplessly on the blanket. "I suppose he might have an allergy to something not connected with the food."

Where is that ambulance? Nancy thought to herself. If it takes much longer . . . She didn't finish her thought. She was terribly afraid of what might happen if Alexander continued to cough and thrash around so violently.

"A cousin of mine had an allergy to bees and used to get really sick when she got stung," Bess said. "Could it have been something like that?"

"That's a possibility," Ted said. "Or maybe a spider bite."

"I don't know," Nancy said doubtfully. "I don't think either of those two allergies would cause coughing."

Keiko had become very quiet when Alexander collapsed. Her eyes were now wide with terror. "What's happening to us?" she whispered.

Ted put an arm around her shoulders. "Keiko, I'm sure this has nothing to do with what happened to you."

I'm not so sure he's right, Nancy thought. Two unexplained incidents in one morning were a bit too much of a coincidence. Alarm bells were ringing loudly in her head. Was someone out to get the piano finalists?

The ambulance arrived with its siren shrieking. A path was cleared through the crowd of concertgoers directly to Alexander. Two emergency service attendants rolled a gurney out of the back of the ambulance and lifted Alexander onto it. They positioned an oxygen mask over his face, which didn't stop the coughing but did seem to calm him slightly.

Nancy, Bess, and Ted all decided to follow the ambulance to the local hospital in Nancy's car. Keiko excused herself, saying that she preferred to lie down for a while. She left for the dorm on the far side of the Great Lawn as the ambulance pulled away. Poor thing, Nancy thought. This has been too much for her.

When Nancy turned into the parking lot of the Westbridge Hospital, she could see Alexander being lifted out of the ambulance. Attendants quickly wheeled the gurney through the emergency entrance. An emergency room nurse steered him to a curtained cubicle, quickly followed by a doctor on call. Ted, Bess, and Nancy sat in the waiting area just outside the cubicle. Almost immediately, the coughing subsided, and there was an ominous silence.

Bess looked fearfully at Nancy. "Do you think he's all right?" she asked.

"I don't know, but I guess we'll find out soon," Nancy said nervously.

Ted stood up and waited next to the curtained area. His face was drawn and pale. The thought flashed through Nancy's mind that he was the only one of the three finalists who hadn't been hurt. She knew this meant that he was a possible suspect but couldn't believe he'd done these awful things.

If he wasn't guilty, that meant he was probably in danger. A sudden wave of apprehension washed over Nancy. What else could go wrong? How could Ted be hurt? She became even more determined to find out what was going on.

As the doctor emerged unexpectedly from the examining room, he almost tripped over Ted.

"Oh, there you are," he said, regaining his balance. "Are you all here with this boy?"

"Yes," Ted said. "What happened to him? Will he be all right?"

"Yes, he'll be fine. He has a bad case of food poisoning, but we've pumped his stomach and given him something to calm the intestinal tract. He'll sleep for a while, but then he can go home." The doctor reached into the breast pocket of his white coat and took out a small white pad and ballpoint pen. "I'll need some details about what he ate today. Can any of you help with that?"

Reaching into her shoulder bag, Nancy withdrew the box of mushroom salad and the roll, which she had wrapped in a napkin. She handed them to the doctor.

"This is what Alexander was eating just before he got sick," Nancy explained.

The doctor nodded. "It's very good that you brought this with you. We'll run some tests." The doctor called for a lab technician to pick up the food samples.

Then he turned to Nancy, Bess, and Ted. "Your friend will be moved to a more comfortable bed in a separate room while he recovers," he explained. "In the meantime, could you sign him in at the front desk? I'll be around to check on him in a little while."

He was already attending to his next patient,

checking the pulse of a young woman who appeared to be unconscious.

"Boy, it never stops around here," Bess said. "Emergency room doctors must be exhausted at the end of the day."

The woman behind the admitting desk smiled at Bess as she handed her a form attached to a clipboard. "This is a relatively slow day," she said. "You should see it when the tourist season really gets under way, in August."

Ted stood by and watched as Alexander was wheeled from the examining room. He seemed to be sleeping, clearly exhausted from his ordeal. Turning to Bess and Nancy, Ted said, "I'm going with him. I want to make sure he doesn't get too upset when he wakes up in a hospital room alone."

"That's a good idea," Nancy said. "We'll join you as soon as we call someone at the festival to fill out this form. They have to be notified of his condition, anyway."

Ted took off after the attendant, who had just wheeled Alexander through the double doors leading from the emergency room to another wing of the hospital.

After Nancy made the phone call to the festival, she turned to Bess and said tensely, "I don't like this."

"I know. You're thinking that it's too much of a coincidence, aren't you?" Bess asked.

Nancy nodded grimly. "It seems that someone is trying to eliminate each of the finalists, one by one."

"But whoever it is isn't succeeding. Keiko will be able to practice by tomorrow. . . ."

"We hope," Nancy reminded her.

"And Alexander should be okay after he sleeps for a while," Bess said. When Nancy didn't respond, Bess looked at her friend anxiously. "Shouldn't he?"

Nancy was frowning distractedly, staring at the double doors where Ted had just disappeared. Finally, she nodded slowly. "Yes, Alexander and Keiko will both probably be all right. But what about Ted? Since we don't know why this is being done, or who's doing it, anything could happen to him."

"But what can we do?" Bess asked. "Without a bodyguard, anybody could get to Ted." She grinned suddenly. "Unless, of course, you'd like to volunteer for the job."

Nancy blushed, then said hurriedly, "I think we should discuss what we know and try to figure out the motivation and the possible culprits."

When Bess agreed, Nancy added, "But first I think we'd better talk to Alexander. Maybe he can add something to what we already know."

When the festival official arrived, Nancy and Bess went to Alexander's room on the third floor.

As they entered Room 343, Alexander was sitting up in bed and Ted was rearranging his pillows. The Russian pianist acted embarrassed when he saw Nancy and Bess.

"I must thank you for helping me," Alexander began awkwardly.

"We're just relieved you're all right," Nancy said reassuringly.

"Yes," Bess added. "You had us scared."

"I'm really very healthy. There was no need to worry," Alexander said, still quite pale. He sighed and settled back against the pillows.

"I was wondering if you had any ideas about what caused your food poisoning," Nancy said.

"It could not have been the mushrooms, this I know," Alexander said emphatically. "I gathered them myself in the woods near the festival grounds. I know mushrooms very well, and I would never have picked a poisonous one by mistake. Never." He began to breathe heavily, and Ted touched him gently on the shoulder.

"Take it easy, Alex," he said. "I'm sure it wasn't the mushrooms."

At that moment a doctor walked in. "I'm afraid I must disagree with your diagnosis," he said to Alexander. "The tests we've run show conclusively that your salad included an extremely poisonous type of mushroom."

# Chapter Five

IMPOSSIBLE! I tell you, this cannot be," Alexander shouted, rising up on one arm and turning red in the face. "I picked those mushrooms myself."

The doctor moved swiftly to the bed and eased Alexander back against the pillows. "Try to calm down," he said. "Let's see if we can get to the bottom of this.

"There is one poisonous mushroom in particular that grows wild around here," the doctor said. "It's grayish white. Although it usually takes several hours to cause a reaction when eaten, it has been known to happen much faster. You could easily have mistaken an *Amanita phalloides* for a nonpoisonous mushroom if you were in those woods over near the festival."

"No, I saw nothing like what you describe. Nothing," Alexander insisted.

"Wait a minute," Nancy interjected. "When did you pack your picnic lunch? I mean, did you prepare the mushroom salad earlier this morning and then refrigerate it until lunchtime?"

Alexander stared at Nancy with narrowed eyes. "Yes," he said slowly. "That is exactly what I did. I made the salad around eight o'clock, just after I picked the mushrooms. Then I left it in the dorm refrigerator until lunchtime. What are you saying—that someone poisoned my lunch on purpose?"

"I'm not sure what happened," Nancy said, "but we can't rule anything out. If you're sure you didn't pick any poisonous mushrooms—"

"I'm sure!" Alexander shouted.

"Then I think we have to consider the possibility that someone tampered with your food."

At this point the doctor spoke up. "I think Alexander needs to rest. He's had a pretty rough time today. Why don't you come back later, when he's had some sleep?" He ushered them from the room.

Closing Alexander's door, he turned to face Nancy, Bess, and Ted, his expression serious.

"You've just come to a pretty dramatic conclusion without having much to go on. What makes you certain he didn't pick a bad mushroom himself?"

Nancy filled him in on Alexander's knowledge of mushrooms. The doctor listened. When she'd finished, he said, "I see. But why would someone want to hurt this young man?"

"We'd better tell him what's been happening," Ted said anxiously. He explained who he was to the doctor, and said that it was possible that someone was trying to hurt the finalists in the piano competition.

"This is a shocking story," the doctor said. "I think you'd better get in touch with the police. If you really believe that Alexander was poisoned deliberately, I'll have to inform them."

Nancy thought this over for a moment, "I think we should wait. Maybe you're right—this could be just a coincidence. I'm not comfortable involving the police until we know more."

Ted nodded slowly. "It's possible Alexander doesn't know as much about mushrooms as he says. There's no proof that he didn't pick the poisonous one himself." It seemed to Nancy that he was trying hard to convince himself that it had been an accident.

The doctor sighed. "All right. We'll leave it

for now. But if you decide later that you feel there was malicious intent involved here, promise me that you'll let the police know immediately." He reached into his breast pocket and withdrew a card with his name printed on it: Dr. Charles Hartill, Department of Toxicology. "Will you get in touch with me if you have any more trouble?"

Nancy nodded. This man seemed genuinely concerned, and she was grateful for his professional point of view.

As the trio headed back to the festival in Nancy's car, they discussed the events of the day.

"I can't believe someone actually is trying to harm us," Ted said.

"Who would benefit if the finalists were unable to play?" Nancy asked.

"Well, there are the semifinalists who were just eliminated. They're still here in case something happens to us," Ted said, frowning.

"You mean, if a finalist were unable to compete, a semifinalist would be brought in to replace him or her?" Bess asked.

Ted nodded. "That's right."

"How many semifinalists are there?" Nancy asked.

"Two," Ted said. "And I know them both from other competitions. They're okay. They'd never try anything like this."

"How can you be so sure?" Bess asked. "You yourself were saying how fierce the competition can be and how a pianist needs to win one of these contests to have a successful career."

Ted didn't reply for several minutes. He turned away and looked out the window at the passing landscape, illuminated by the afternoon sun. Finally, he spoke. "Look, I just can't believe anyone I know personally would do something like this."

"Maybe we should drop it for now," Nancy said quietly. "We can talk about it later, if you like."

Ted nodded, his expression gloomy. "How about doing something completely unmusical this afternoon?" he said.

"What did you have in mind?" Nancy asked.

"I know of a beautiful lake not too far from here. It's great for swimming, and they rent small sailboats. How about it?"

"That sounds wonderful," Bess said.

"I love to sail," Nancy said, "and I haven't been in ages." Looking at the clock on the dashboard, she added, "It's only three-thirty now, so there's plenty of time before dinner. We just have to pick up our bathing suits at Mrs. Wheeler's, and then we can go."

Ted said, "Great. I'll be fine swimming in my cutoffs."

After the girls changed at Mrs. Wheeler's, they drove to Lake Poconset. It was a large lake, ringed with tall pine trees and an occasional dock. Several people were out in small boats. The sails were colorful, and the boats zigzagged on the lake, making a brilliant patchwork pattern.

"I knew this was a good idea," Ted said. Nancy was glad to see that he was beginning to cheer up. In a lower voice, he added, "The two semifinalists are here. I guess they didn't go to the concert. I'll introduce you."

He led Nancy and Bess toward a young man and woman sitting in beach chairs and reading. They looked up as Ted called their names.

"Jean-Claude, Maura! I want you to meet some friends of mine—Nancy Drew and Bess Marvin." The two pianists stood up to shake hands, then gestured for the newcomers to sit on the blanket that was on the sand next to their chairs. Before sitting, Ted quickly explained what had happened to Alex and Keiko and assured them that they would be all right.

Nancy sat next to Maura MacDonald, a Scots girl with flaming red hair, deep blue eyes, and freckles. She was wearing a black tank suit.

Jean-Claude Pascal had thick dark hair, dark eyes, and a penetrating gaze. Nancy could see that Bess was immediately drawn to his brooding good looks and his French accent. Nancy had to admit that he was handsome, even though he wasn't exactly her type. He seemed slightly moody, though he looked like a French movie star.

"What are you doing taking time off from your practice schedule?" Maura asked Ted sharply. Nancy thought Maura sounded cold and unfriendly.

"I've switched over to early morning practice," Ted said casually. He didn't seem to be fazed by her tone. "And after what happened today, I need to rest and skip my second practice."

"I hate early morning practices," Jean-Claude said in his deep voice. "Getting up at the crack of dawn—I can't stand it!"

"If I were you, I'd be getting in all the practice I could," Maura said to Ted, her eyes narrowing. "You haven't won yet, you know."

Ted smiled warily. "Don't worry, Maura. I'm putting in my hours."

Nancy was struck by the girl's obvious hostility. She seemed to have a bad case of sour grapes.

Shading his eyes and looking out at the boats on the lake, Ted asked, "Is anyone up for a sail?"

"Count me in," Nancy said.

"Not me," Jean-Claude said. "I'm not much

of a swimmer, and I never learned how to sail. I just like lying in the sun near the water."

Maura marked her place in the book she was reading and stood up. "I'd like to come, too, if it's all right with you." She eyed Ted doubtfully, but he smiled at her and nodded.

"Sure," he said. "How about you, Bess?"

"No, thanks," Bess said. "I'm not much of a sailor, and I'd probably just get in the way. Besides," she added, stretching out on the blanket, "I wouldn't mind getting some sun."

Nancy grinned to herself. She had been sailing with Bess many times. She knew that Bess just wanted to stay behind and talk with Jean-Claude.

Ted, Maura, and Nancy selected a large sunfish from the rental place at the end of the dock. They headed out onto the lake with Ted at the tiller and Nancy and Maura taking the sail.

There was a good breeze, and the boat picked up speed right away. They all began to relax and enjoy the ride. It had been a hot day, and the cool air felt refreshing.

Ted put his arm around Nancy's shoulders so casually that at first she didn't notice it. When she did, it was with a sensation of real pleasure. She felt as if she'd known him for a long time, not just one day. She felt relaxed with his arm around her.

Ted began a story about the first time he'd gone sailing alone near Catalina Island, off the California coast. He was just describing a sudden storm when Maura let out a piercing scream.

"Look out," she shouted, pointing behind them. Nancy and Ted looked around to see another boat bearing down on them. The two boats were about to crash!

# Chapter Six

"JUMP!" Ted and Nancy yelled simultaneous ly. The three managed to jump overboard and swim clear of the area just as the two boats collided.

They treaded water, watching with shock as both boats capsized and began to sink.

"That was close!" Ted exclaimed.

"Do either of you see who was in the other boat?" Nancy asked. "I hope he or she wasn't injured."

"No, I didn't notice," Ted replied. Maura shook her head.

Suddenly Nancy noticed another head bobbing nearby in the water—that of a dark-haired man. When he turned around and faced her, she could see it was Jean-Claude.

At that moment a lifeguard sped up in a motorboat. He helped all four sailors on board, handing each an orange life jacket for the trip back to shore. He made sure they put them on and tied them securely.

"You should have been wearing these when you took the boats out. Didn't anyone at the boat rental make sure you had them?" he asked, surprised.

"No," Ted replied sheepishly. "Of course you're right, and I should have known. It never occurred to me."

Ted suddenly seemed to register Jean-Claude's presence and turned to stare at him. "Were you sailing that other boat?" he asked.

Jean-Claude was obviously embarrassed. "Yes," he said, not meeting Ted's eyes.

"But why did you take a boat out? I thought you said you didn't know how to sail," Nancy said, frowning.

Jean-Claude cleared his throat noisily and looked away. "I wanted to take a boat out on my own." Seeing the shocked expressions on their faces, he added defensively, "I do know how to sail—a bit."

"A bit is right," shouted Ted. "You could have gotten us all killed!"

"You exaggerate," Jean-Claude said coolly. Nancy couldn't believe what she was hearing

—Jean-Claude seemed unwilling to take responsibility for what had just happened.

Maura spoke up for the first time since the accident. "This is all your fault," she said to Jean-Claude angrily. "You don't know how to sail, if that was an example of what you know." She stopped, squeezing out her dripping red hair. "But I think you do know how to swim. . . ."

It was true, Nancy thought. Jean-Claude had said he wasn't much of a swimmer, but when she'd seen him in the water, he was doing just fine. What is going on here? she wondered. Is it possible he aimed his boat deliberately at us?

Maura turned to Ted and touched him on the arm. "This accident was not your fault," she said. "He gave you no time to steer out of the way." She glared at Jean-Claude for emphasis.

When the motorboat pulled up to the dock, the lifeguard had them all sign accident reports. Since no one was willing to charge Jean-Claude with reckless endangerment, the report wouldn't go any further than the lake patrol and the boat rental's insurance company. No one really wanted to involve the police and possibly get Jean-Claude into trouble. After all, Nancy reasoned, Jean-Claude claimed it was an accident. Maybe it was.

As Nancy explained to Bess what had happened, she found herself wondering just how much of an accident it had actually been. She watched out of the corner of her eye as Maura and Jean-Claude drove off. The semifinalists in this competition were bound to be pretty resentful, she thought. Maybe one of them was resentful enough to cause the "accidents" that kept occurring. Nancy hoped they'd find out more once she and Bess moved into the festival dorm.

After dropping Ted off at his dorm, Nancy and Bess continued on to Mrs. Wheeler's. It had been an unusually eventful day, and they both felt the need to unwind.

Mrs. Wheeler greeted them warmly. She was in her early fifties but seemed younger because of her athletic build and short, thick light brown hair. Nancy found herself responding gratefully to her no-nonsense air and her intelligence. Nancy and Bess filled her in on the day's events as they sat down to dinner.

The next morning, Saturday, Nancy and Bess returned to the festival dorm after an early breakfast to look for Ted and Keiko. They were directed to the common room, a large airy space with comfortable armchairs and sofas. The walls were decorated with concert posters and photographs of famous musicians who had played at the festival.

The room was dominated by a black grand piano that stood in one corner. Keiko was playing scales up and down the length of the keyboard with thunderous speed.

When Nancy and Bess approached, Keiko's face lit up. She finished a scale with a dramatic flourish and smiled radiantly, holding up her wrist for their inspection.

"Look," she said happily. "Just like the doctor said. No problems."

"That's wonderful news, Keiko!" Nancy said. "You're amazing," Bess added. "I can't wait to hear you play your concerto with the orchestra."

Keiko grinned. "You will on Monday afternoon. I had my final rehearsal with the orchestra this morning, playing on the actual piano we'll be using. I think it went really well. The conductor helped me block out my performance, and I know this piece so thoroughly I could play it in my sleep."

"What does it mean to block out your performance?" Bess asked.

"The conductor lets me know how he plans to approach the music. For instance, he told me today exactly how long he wants me to wait before joining in after the orchestra plays the introduction, and how he wants to pace the piece section by section." Noticing their puzzled expressions, she added, "It's complicated, but you'll see what I mean when you hear me play the concerto. It's really just the conductor's way of coordinating the orchestra with the soloist so we play smoothly together."

Bess said, "I wish I'd had piano lessons when I was younger. It must be wonderful to be able to play like you do."

Keiko smiled. "I have to admit, I love it."

Just then Ted walked into the common room. He was wearing faded jeans and a blue T-shirt. He greeted all of them and gave Nancy a warm smile.

"I'm glad you're here," he said. "I was just going to find the dorm supervisor to ask about that room for you and Bess. If you'll stick around for a while, we may be able to take care of it this morning."

"I think that's a good idea," Nancy said. "We discussed it with Mrs. Wheeler last night, and she was very understanding."

As Nancy was talking, the door swung open and Jean-Claude entered the common room. He was wearing sunglasses, black jeans, and a white festival T-shirt. He acknowledged their presence with a quick nod, then sat on a sofa on the other side of the room. He chose a music magazine from several that were scattered on a low table, and started to read.

Bess's eyes lit up when she saw the French pianist. "I think it will be great to stay here," she said. Catching sight of Nancy's knowing smile, she blushed and added, "I mean, we'll have a better chance of finding out what's happening if we're on the scene, right?"

Nancy squeezed her friend's arm affectionately. "Yes, we will," she said.

"Good," Ted said. "I'll see what I can work out."

After he'd gone, Keiko joined Nancy and Bess, and the three girls settled into comfortable armchairs in a corner of the room.

"Keiko," Nancy began, keeping her voice low, "do the semifinalists usually stay around after they've been eliminated in case one of the finalists drops out?"

"They can if they want to," Keiko said thoughtfully. "But technically, they're not required to stay. I know, because I've been a semifinalist myself."

"Did you stay on after you were eliminated?" Bess asked.

"No. I couldn't stand being around the finalists, so I went home," Keiko admitted, smiling ruefully. "But I know some people do stay on. Maybe it's partly because they came so close and can't bear to leave." She shrugged. "It's different for each of us. We all have our own ways of dealing with failure, I guess."

The pianist seemed to be lost in her own

thoughts for a moment. "Actually, I've been wanting to talk to you about something I remembered last night. I was at a competition in England last year, and one of the semifinalists got food poisoning."

"Really?" Nancy asked eagerly. "Tell me what you remember."

"Well, the person it happened to is here this year. She was one of the semifinalists last year and this year, too," Keiko began. "Her name is Maura MacDonald."

"We met her yesterday," Nancy said excitedly. "She and Jean-Claude were at the lake when we went sailing."

At the mention of his name, the French pianist looked up briefly, then went back to his reading. Nancy resolved to keep her voice even lower.

"Oh, yes, I heard about your accident," Keiko said. "Thank goodness you were all right!"

Nancy nodded. "Did anyone else come down with food poisoning at the same time? Or just Maura?"

"That's what was so mysterious about it," Keiko replied. "Everyone ate in the same cafeteria because the competition was sponsored by Cambridge University. And no one else got sick."

"Did they find out what made her sick?" Nancy asked.

"I'm afraid I don't know any details," Keiko said apologetically. "I had already left when the incident occurred. I was not one of the semifinalists."

"Perhaps I can help," a deep voice said. Jean-Claude had suddenly appeared behind Keiko's chair and was hovering uncertainly.

"Hello, Jean-Claude," Bess said. "Why don't you join us?"

"I'm sorry to interrupt, but I heard you speaking of Cambridge and Maura's food poisoning." He seemed anxious not to be blamed for eavesdropping.

Nancy felt annoyed. She thought that Jean-Claude couldn't have heard their conversation unless he'd made a deliberate effort to do so. Why would he listen in? she wondered. "Why don't you pull up a chair and join us?" she said graciously, hiding her annoyance.

"Thank you, I will." The French pianist sat down. "It's just that I was there, too, you see," he said.

"Of course!" Keiko said. "You were one of the semifinalists in Cambridge as well."

"Yes," Jean-Claude said. "Anyway, as Keiko told you, no one else got sick, and it was extremely mysterious. But I know Maura can tell you more about it."

"Do you know where she is now?" asked Nancy.

"Yes, I do. She always practices at this time in one of the practice rooms," he replied.

"The building is across the Great Lawn, beyond the orchestra shell," Keiko explained.

"Let's go see if we can find her," Nancy said, getting up quickly. She paused. "Should we wait until she's finished practicing? She might not want to be interrupted."

"It's almost ten o'clock," Jean-Claude said, looking at his watch. "I know she usually takes a break at ten. I think it should be okay."

"I'd better take you to the practice rooms," Keiko said. "That building is like a maze, and you'll never find her on your own."

"If you don't mind, I'll stay here. I am waiting for a phone call," Jean-Claude said.

Noticing a familiar infatuated expression on Bess's face, Nancy said, "Bess, why don't you wait here for Ted? He should be back soon. I don't want him to think we took off without finding out about the dorm room."

"Sure, Nan," Bess said. "I'll just read some magazines."

The last thing Nancy saw as she and Keiko left the room was Bess turning to Jean-Claude and striking up a conversation. Nancy smiled to herself.

On the way to the practice rooms, Nancy

and Keiko discussed Maura and Jean-Claude. Nancy asked if Keiko thought they were good pianists.

"Well, of course they're both good enough to get this far," Keiko explained, "which means they stand out from other pianists in their age group. The problem is, they each have handicaps that have gotten in the way of their making it to the finals."

"Can you tell me a bit more?" Nancy asked.

"Sure. In Jean-Claude's case, it's pretty easy to see why he's never been a finalist. He's a very flashy pianist, with amazing technique. He always chooses the most difficult music to play, and the judges are always impressed by his ability."

"So what's the problem?" Nancy asked.

"His problem is what the judges call musicianship, which means his interpretation of the music. He doesn't pour enough feeling into his performance, so it always sounds a bit mechanical in the end." She sighed. "It's so hard to learn to balance the two. I guess he just spent a lot of time perfecting his technique, and he sort of lost out on the emotional side."

"Couldn't his teachers have pointed out the problem to him along the way?" Nancy asked.

"They probably tried to, but in the end, a pianist is capable of playing only what he himself—or she herself—feels."

"And what about Maura?" Nancy asked. "Why has she never been a finalist?"

"That's harder to pin down," Keiko said. "I think it's just a question of luck in her case. Luck and time. She's very good. She'll be a finalist eventually. It just hasn't happened yet."

"Is that why she's so bitter?" Nancy asked.

Keiko nodded. "So you've noticed Ms. MacDonald's temper. Yes, I'd say she realizes she's just as good as the finalists, and she thinks she's been passed over unfairly."

As they entered the building, they could hear the faint sound of piano music coming through the thick walls. Keiko led Nancy down the stairs to a basement level, which housed most of the practice rooms. They passed room after room, looking through the small eye-level windows in the doors.

Finally they found Maura. So as not to break her concentration, Nancy and Keiko waited patiently for her to stop playing before they knocked. As she listened, Nancy could hear that Maura was very accomplished. She was playing a Chopin waltz, and Nancy found the music sad and beautiful at the same time. Nancy thought the deeply felt rendition was probably what Keiko meant by musicianship.

When the last note had died away, Keiko knocked softly.

"Come in," Maura called. She smiled at them and said happily, "I've had a really good morning."

"I'm glad to see you've recovered from our accident yesterday," Nancy said.

"Oh, yes, wasn't that stupid?" Maura said, frowning. "I really let Jean-Claude have it afterward. Honestly, he can be such a fool sometimes."

"So, you don't think the accident was deliberate?" Nancy asked slowly.

The Scottish pianist stared at her. "What do you mean?"

"Well, you know what happened to Keiko yesterday morning," Nancy began. Keiko held up her hand, pointing out the slight bruising that remained. "And then Alexander was poisoned by bad mushrooms," Nancy continued.

Maura nodded. "So you think someone's out to get the finalists—and the sailing accident was another attack?" She looked skeptical. "I think Jean-Claude did something foolish, not deliberate."

Nancy and Keiko looked at each other, as if trying to decide whether to bring up the subject they had been discussing earlier. "Keiko told me that you had food poisoning yourself at the Cambridge competition last year," Nancy said cautiously.

Maura shuddered. "Yes, it was horrible."

"Did they ever determine how you were poisoned?"

"They said it was a piece of bad fish. But I don't see how it could have been, since we all ate the same fish, and no one else got sick," Maura explained.

"Which of the pianists who are here now were in England last year?" Nancy asked.

Maura stared at Keiko. "We all were," she said slowly. "Weren't we?"

Keiko nodded. "That's right. Jean-Claude and Alexander were there, and Maura and I. Ted was there, too."

"You mean the exact same group of finalists and semifinalists were at that contest?" Nancy asked. "Isn't that an amazing coincidence?"

"It wasn't quite the same," Maura explained. "We were all semifinalists last year. It was a different contest with different rules. There were six semifinalists and three finalists."

Nancy absorbed this information. So one year had made the difference for Keiko, Alexander, and Ted, she realized. They had gone from semifinalist to finalist status. But Jean-Claude and Maura had not been so lucky. That must have been a huge disappointment for them, Nancy thought.

"Keiko left Cambridge before you got sick," Nancy said. "Had the others stayed around?"

"Yes, everyone else stayed on," Maura replied. "We were all curious to see who would win."

Just then there was a knock at the door, and Ted and Bess came in.

"Hi!" Bess said. "Ted found out that we can have a room beginning tonight if we want it, and we came to tell you the good news," Bess said.

"That's great!" Nancy said.

"It's a beautiful morning," Ted said. "I thought it might be fun to go for a hike on some of the mountain trails nearby. Is anyone up for that?"

Maura and Keiko both said they had too much to do.

"It sounds like fun to me," Nancy said. "I'd love to see some of the countryside." She looked at Bess. "What do you think?" she asked.

"Well," Bess started slowly, "Jean-Claude mentioned something about an open rehearsal now, and I sort of thought I'd like to hear that. Would you mind if I didn't come?"

"Those rehearsals are great," Ted said encouragingly. "You'll enjoy it."

"Go for it!" Nancy said with a smile.

Bess laughed, relieved. "Okay."

Maura went back to her practicing, and Keiko left to pick up some music from another practice room. Ted, Nancy, and Bess walked out together and made their way across the Great Lawn toward the orchestra shell. Bess waited there for Jean-Claude, and Ted and Nancy continued on together.

"Alone at last!" Ted said with a twinkle in his eye.

Nancy blushed. "Yes! I'm ready for our great adventure. How do we get to the mountain trail?" she asked.

"Let's take my bike," Ted suggested. "First let me get a sweater from my room. You're dressed for this," he explained, indicating Nancy's yellow crewneck sweater and jeans, "but I'm not. I can't seem to get used to the weather here. It's not California, that's for sure!" he said with a grin. They walked to the dorm, and Nancy waited in the common room while Ted went for his sweater.

After twenty minutes had passed, Nancy was just about to start searching for him when the door burst open and Ted stumbled into the room. There was blood on his face and hands!

# Chapter Seven

"WHAT HAPPENED?" Nancy cried as she ran to Ted's side. He collapsed against her, and she slowly led him to a chair.

Sitting down beside him, she examined the side of his head along the hairline. When she pulled her hand away, she noticed a trace of blood.

"We've got to get you to a doctor right away," she said firmly. "You have a head wound of some kind, and there's no telling how serious it is."

Ted held up his hands. "Wait," he said. "Let me—just let me pull myself together." He sat silently for a moment. "I think I'll be okay. Really."

Nancy wasn't convinced but decided not to

insist while he was so badly shaken. Instead, she said quietly, "Tell me what happened."

"I went to my room, just down the hall." Ted pointed behind him. "The door was unlocked, so I should have known right away that something was wrong."

He paused and Nancy took his hand and squeezed it gently. "Go on," she said.

"When I walked in, I couldn't see anything because the shades were drawn and my eyes weren't adjusted to the dark," Ted continued. "Someone must have been hiding behind the door, and as soon as I moved toward the window to open the shades, whoever it was hit me on the head."

Nancy looked at her watch. It was eleven. "I think we should call the police and let them know what happened," she said firmly. "You didn't see who it was, I'm sure, but maybe your attacker left a clue."

Ted shook his head. "I feel like such a fool." Then he sat up straight. "Let's not call the police. Let's go check out my room right now."

"Do you think this person was after something?" Nancy asked.

"Could be," Ted said. "Anyway, I don't want to wait." As he stood up shakily, Nancy grabbed his arm to steady him.

"Take it easy," she said. "You've just been hit on the head." Together they walked down the corridor to Ted's room. When they reached it, the door was still open. Ted walked in slowly, and Nancy followed.

"Don't touch anything," she said quickly. "There may be fingerprints."

"But I need to check to see what's missing," Ted said. "What if I use a tissue or a towel?"

"Yes, that would probably be all right," Nancy replied. She moved to the windows and opened the shades, which were still drawn. The room was immediately flooded with light.

The room had been ransacked. Loose pages of music were strewn over every surface. The dresser drawers had been pulled out and their contents dumped on the floor. "Looks like the intruder meant business," Ted said grimly.

"But what could he or she have been after?" Nancy asked. "Do you suppose the person wanted to wreck your room to upset you before your performance Monday?"

Without answering, Ted ran to the night table next to his bed. Wrapping his hand in a T-shirt from the pile on the floor, he pulled out the drawer. It was empty. He stared at it for a long moment. "I don't believe it," he said finally.

Nancy hurried to his side and touched his arm. "What is it? What did they get?" she asked.

"My notated score from the conductor,"

Ted said. Noticing the puzzled expression on Nancy's face, he added, "The orchestra notes for my concerto performance on Monday."

"You mean someone stole your score? But why would they bother to do that? Aren't there other copies of it?" Nancy asked.

Ted sat down in the armchair near the window. He touched the spot on his head that had been bleeding, then looked at his hand. Nancy quickly found a clean towel in the jumble of clothes on the floor and pressed it to his scalp.

Ted looked at her gratefully. "Yes, there are other copies. But I had made notes on my score, and there are no copies of those." He put his head in his hands.

"But will this really spoil your performance?" Nancy asked. "I'm sure you know the music inside out. Couldn't you piece together your notes from memory? Or could you talk to the conductor about what happened and get his help?"

"Sure, I could do that," Ted said, "but it won't be the same. Those notes are a key part of a good performance. I would have used them to practice with right up until the actual performance on Monday."

He paused. "And, sure, maybe the conductor will sit down with me and talk me through the concerto, but I doubt it. Right now his time is too valuable. He's also conducting the festival orchestra's daily concerts."

Nancy hadn't known this. What a terrible thing to happen to Ted, she thought. There was no longer any doubt in her mind: someone was trying to sabotage the finalists, and it seemed they had succeeded.

Suddenly Nancy noticed something shiny lying on the floor near the door. Using a washcloth, she picked it up and examined it. It was a small heavy metal object, triangular in shape, with a separate rod attached.

"What's a metronome doing over there?" Ted said. "Can I see it?"

Nancy handed it to him. "Be careful," she said. "There may be fingerprints."

"Do you think this is what he—whoever—used to hit me?" Ted asked.

Nancy frowned. "There's doesn't seem to be any blood on it, but we should definitely have it examined by the police to see what they turn up." She looked at the messy room. "Is there a housekeeper on staff in this dorm, or do the musicians clean their own rooms?"

"There's a housekeeper," Ted said. "It's very luxurious—someone makes the beds every morning."

"Good," Nancy said. "Someone will help you straighten the room—later, of course, after it's been dusted for fingerprints. First, let's ask the staff nurse to take a look at you. Then I'll call the police."

Ted and Nancy had to walk through the common room to get to the nurse's office. As they entered the room, Bess was entering from the opposite side.

"Nan!" she shouted gaily. She stopped smiling when she saw that Ted was holding a towel to his head.

"Are you all right?" she asked him. "What happened?"

"It's a long story," Nancy said. "I'm just walking Ted to the nurse's office, and then you and I can call the police. Will you wait for me here?"

"Sure," Bess said.

"Listen, Nancy," Ted put in. "I can find the nurse on my own. And I can also alert festival security about what happened. I know they like to take care of things their own way, and they'd get very annoyed if we took the matter into our own hands." He held up the metronome, still wrapped in the washcloth.

He touched Nancy's arm gently. "Really, I'll be all right." He frowned at the metronome, then at Nancy, a confused expression on his face. "It's just that this seems—I'm not sure, but it looks familiar."

Nancy looked at him with curiosity. "Aren't there a lot of metronomes here? Is this one unusual in some way?"

"No, it's not that," Ted said slowly. "But most of the metronomes are in the practice rooms, not here in the dorm. And I seem to remember this one from somewhere. If I could only think clearly," he added, touching the side of his head. "I know I'll remember if I think about it."

Nancy studied his face anxiously. "Why don't you let me talk to security while you go see the nurse? I really think you should lie down for a while."

Ted nodded and explained where the security office was located. Handing Nancy the metronome, he stared at it, his eyes narrowed. Finally he shook his head and said, "I'm sorry about our hike, Nancy—maybe we can do it some other time." He gave Nancy and Bess a strained smile, then walked off in the direction of the nurse's office.

"Tell me what happened," Bess demanded.

Nancy filled her in as they walked to the security office. "What a morning," she said in a low voice. "At least now I'm convinced that someone is deliberately trying to sabotage all of the finalists."

Bess was appalled. "Does Ted have any idea who might have taken his score?" she asked.

Nancy shook her head. "I don't think so," she said slowly, "though I want to talk to him again when he's had some rest." Eyeing the metronome uneasily, she added, "I've been thinking about this all morning, ever since our conversations with Keiko and Maura. No matter how you look at it, one fact stands out—the people who have the most to gain by sabotaging the finalists are the semifinalists."

They found the security office, but the head of security was out. They explained what had happened to the secretary, filled in a report, and left the metronome behind for the security chief to examine on his return.

As they headed back to the common room, Bess sighed audibly. "I know you're right about the semifinalists, but I don't want to believe it. I know Maura has a temper, but I just can't imagine her cutting Keiko's saddle girth or poisoning Alexander." She bit her lip. "And I also can't believe that Jean-Claude could have done any of those things."

Nancy patted her friend's shoulder as they reached the common room. They found two empty armchairs in a corner of the room, away from some musicians who were engaged in a passionate conversation. "I know you like Jean-Claude," she said, "but the fact remains that both he and Maura had the strongest motive for all of the incidents. And Jean-

Claude did run into us with his sailboat," she added thoughtfully.

Bess leapt to his defense. "That wasn't deliberate," she insisted. "Don't forget, I saw it happen from the beach—he was just trying to sail the boat alone, and he didn't know enough about it. The most he was guilty of was—was—bad judgment," she finished, folding her arms across her chest.

"All right, I believe you. That may have been an accident, but the other incidents definitely weren't."

"So what do we do now?" asked Bess, calming down. "Talk to Maura and Jean-Claude and get their alibis for each of the other incidents?"

"Yes," Nancy said, "that's what we have to do. We have to find out their whereabouts when each accident happened. By the way," she added, "You weren't at the rehearsal very long. What happened?"

"Well, Jean-Claude was bored with the rehearsal and decided to go practice," Bess replied. "I left then, too."

"Do you know what time that was?" Nancy asked.

Bess shook her head. "Not really. About half an hour before I saw you, I think." Her eyes watered, and she looked unhappily at her friend. "Oh, Nan, you don't think he could have hurt Ted, do you?"

Nancy put her arm around Bess. "Look, there's no point in guessing at this stage," she said soothingly. "I think I should talk to Jean-Claude, and you can talk to Maura. We need to know where they each were."

Bess started to object, then said, "You're probably right. I wouldn't be very objective about Jean-Claude. I like him a lot."

"So I've noticed," Nancy said with a grin.

"And what about Ted?" Bess asked, perking up. "I've noticed the two of you getting pretty chummy."

"He's very sweet," Nancy said.

"And gorgeous," Bess added mischievously.

"Okay, he's gorgeous. I admit it. Now I think we should concentrate on finding out who's behind all the accidents," Nancy said, anxious to get started. She was also eager to avoid discussing her feelings about Ted Martinelli until she herself knew how she felt about him. She got up and headed for the door.

"Hold on, Nan," Bess said. "I'm starving, and it's time for lunch. I think we should go back to Mrs. Wheeler's. We did promise we'd have lunch with her and keep her posted on our move to the dorm."

"You're right," Nancy said. "We won't see much of her for a while if we're moving in here. And I have to admit," she added with a laugh, "I'm pretty hungry, too."

As she and Bess headed for the door, the loudspeaker crackled to life.

"Ladies and gentlemen, we have an important announcement to make. One of the judges, Curt Lucas, has withdrawn from the panel because of unavoidable circumstances. He will be replaced by an alternate judge, Grace Hammel."

The common room was suddenly silent. The musicians who had been arguing and laughing stared at one another in amazement.

Panic began to rise in Nancy. Had something happened to Curt Lucas?

# Chapter Eight

THERE WAS A COMMOTION as everyone started talking at once.

"I wonder what that was all about," Bess said.

"It sounds as if the festival's most famous musician has suddenly had to back out of his judging duties," Nancy said. "I hope it was his choice, not because something happened to him." She glanced around at the musicians in the common room. She moved closer to a group of three who were sitting near her and Bess and listened in on their conversation.

"What a fiasco!" a young woman with curly brown hair and glasses was saying. "Why on earth would he leave now? It doesn't make sense."

"Oh, he's such a star," a thin man said bitterly. "This is just spoiled celebrity behavior. He probably found something that paid better and demanded less of his time."

"Don't be silly," said the third in the group, a man in his midthirties with intelligent eyes. He was holding a violin case. "He obviously didn't plan for this to happen. He's been judging the piano competition here for fifteen years."

Tentatively, Nancy made her presence known. "Excuse me, I'm sorry for interrupting—my name is Nancy Drew, and I'm a friend of the piano finalists."

"What, all of them?" the thin man asked. "That's a good trick. How did you manage it?"

"Shut up, Humphrey. Let her speak. Go on," the violinist said, encouraging Nancy.

"Well, I was just wondering who Grace Hammel is. Can you tell me anything about her?"

"Sure," the girl said. "She has a good reputation as a pianist and a teacher. I know she's trained a couple of prizewinners from other competitions."

"And she also runs a music school in California," added the violinist. "A beautiful one, right on the water near Santa Barbara."

Humphrey gave Nancy a cold look. "Anything else you're dying to know?"

"No, thanks," Nancy said, taking Bess's arm and heading for the door. "Let's get out of here," she said in a low voice.

As they were getting into the car, Bess said, "What a weird guy!"

Nancy nodded. "Yes, but thank goodness they're not all like that. Anyway, let's go talk to Mrs. W. and see what she has to say about all of this and about our moving to the dorm. After all, she's been a sponsor of the festival for years. She may have some good insights."

When they arrived at the house, they found Mrs. Wheeler in the kitchen preparing lunch. "Hello, girls! You're just in time for the first corn of the season and some of the grilled chicken we had last night. Anyone interested?"

"Definitely!" Bess said, sitting down at the large oak kitchen table. The room was sunny and comfortable, filled with fresh-cut flowers and bunches of garden herbs that had been hung up to dry. The smell of basil and tarragon filled the air, and Bess sniffed appreciatively.

Mrs. Wheeler was standing at the huge old-fashioned kitchen range, setting a large pot of water on to boil. She handed Bess and Nancy a large paper bag filled with ears of corn. "Would you mind husking these for me?" she asked.

"Not at all," Nancy answered. While she and Bess husked the ears of tender yellow-and-white corn, they filled Mrs. Wheeler in on what had been happening.

"Do you really think someone is deliberately trying to harm the piano finalists?" she asked Nancy.

"Yes, I do," Nancy said. "It's just too much of a coincidence that all three of them have had these 'accidents' over the past couple of days."

Mrs. Wheeler sighed. "This is very serious," she said. "Don't you think you'd better involve the police at this point? I'm responsible for both of you while you're here, and I don't want you—or anyone—to get hurt."

"I've thought about calling in the police," Nancy said. "But nothing can really be proved, except that someone broke into Ted's room and stole his score and that he was hit on the head."

"Well, that's pretty concrete," Mrs. Wheeler insisted. "Can't you tell the police about that?"

"I wanted to, but Ted said the festival security people should be alerted first, and then they would contact the police."

"All right," Mrs. Wheeler said, "as long as someone in authority knows about it. Honestly, I can't remember anything like this ever happening at the festival before. It's terrible! I think you should call your father and tell him."

"I was just thinking the same thing," Nancy said. "I told him I'd call tomorrow night. He's always helpful with things like this and may have a fresh point of view."

"Won't he be worried?" Mrs. Wheeler asked.

"Probably not," Bess chimed in. "Nancy doesn't seem to be a target in this case. Besides, he knows Nancy can take care of herself. She's always getting involved in mysteries wherever she goes. Right, Nan?"

Nancy nodded and sighed. "And I thought this was going to be a quiet vacation in the peaceful Berkshires," she said.

"Well, just use your common sense," Mrs. Wheeler said. "If things seem to be getting out of hand, come and talk to me before doing anything risky."

"Okay," Nancy promised. "We will."

"And one more thing. I'd like to invite you girls to have dinner with me tonight at the Dandelion Inn."

Bess's eyes grew wide. "I've heard of that place. It's the best restaurant in the Berkshires, isn't it?"

Mrs. Wheeler smiled. "That's what they say. I think you'll love it. It's an eighteenth-century inn, and the atmosphere is wonderful."

"Thanks," Nancy said. "We'd love to join you."

Lunch was delicious. As Bess and Nancy helped clear the table, Nancy said, "How about going for a drive before we head back to the dorm? We haven't had much of a chance to look around, and it's such a beautiful day."

"Absolutely," Bess said.

The girls quickly packed their clothes and loaded the suitcases into the trunk of the convertible, then, promising Mrs. Wheeler they'd be careful, took off.

As they drove along Westbridge Road, they passed signs for the dance, theater, and music festivals that made the area famous.

"Dad told me there is so much to do here, we may want to stay all summer," Nancy said. "I know that the town we're entering is known for its antiques. I'd love to find Mrs. Wheeler a thank-you present."

"Let's stop and check out the stores," Bess said enthusiastically. Antique stores, art galleries, and restaurants lined the main street of the quaint village.

"I feel like we've gone back in time," Bess said. "We shouldn't be wearing jeans and T-shirts but long dresses with petticoats and lace-up boots."

"I'm glad we're not wearing that today,

though. We'd be sweltering," Nancy said, finding a parking space.

The two girls wandered along Main Street until they found a store filled with reproductions of Shaker items. "Mrs. Wheeler was telling me about a town near here that's a fully restored Shaker village. It's just the way it was when the Shakers lived there in the nineteenth century," Nancy said.

The two girls spent nearly an hour browsing through the store. They bought dried herbs and spices. Farther down Main Street, Bess found a pair of pewter candlesticks in a store. "I think these will look nice on Mrs. W's dining room table," she said.

They continued along the main street until they came to the Colonial House Inn, a cozy-looking hotel with a gift shop and restaurant. "This looks so quaint," Bess said. "We've got to go in. Besides, I'm dying for a lemonade—that is, if they have it here." She pointed to a sign next to the front door. "This inn was built in 1793."

"Then I guess we'll have a glass of old-fashioned lemonade," Nancy said with a laugh.

The two girls walked though the lobby to the large sun-filled dining room. They were seated at a high-backed booth overlooking a courtyard.

As they sipped their lemonades, they gazed out the window and took in the buzz of conversation around them. "This is great," Bess said with a contented sigh. "I could sit here for the rest of the day."

Nancy was about to reply when she heard a voice at the next table.

"Ted Martinelli must be happy about this change in judges," the voice said. "Everyone knows that he and Lucas don't get along."

# Chapter Nine

NANCY FROZE when she heard Ted's name mentioned. The voice sounded familiar, and by leaning out and peeking around the side of the booth, she could see that it belonged to Maura MacDonald.

Just as Nancy was wondering how to approach the pianist, Maura and her friend stood up and moved toward the door. Nancy followed the two girls out of the restaurant while Bess paid for their drinks.

"Maura," Nancy called as they emerged into the sunshine.

Startled, the pianist turned back to Nancy. "Oh, hello," she said.

"Hi," Nancy said. "Can I talk to you for a few minutes?"

The pianist shrugged. "Why not?" she said.

"I heard you discussing something that interests me, and I wanted to ask you about it," Nancy began.

Maura and her friend exchanged a tension-filled look. Nancy decided to try to ease the atmosphere by introducing herself to Maura's friend.

"We haven't met. I'm Nancy Drew, and this is my friend Bess Marvin," she added as Bess joined them.

Maura's companion was a tall girl with a friendly smile. "I'm Abby Fisher," she said pleasantly.

"Abby's a pianist, too," Maura said. "She's here to keep me company until the final performances on Monday."

This gave Nancy the opening she needed to bring up what she had overheard.

"I didn't mean to listen in, but your voice carried. What did you mean about Ted and Curt Lucas not getting along?" she asked.

Maura shrugged. "It's no secret. Curt Lucas was the judge of a California competition a couple of years ago, and Ted came in second. He was furious and blamed it on Lucas."

"How do you know this?" Nancy asked.

"Everyone knows," Abby said. "It's just one of those stories that gets around. You know how these things happen. You have a private conversation with someone, and the next day the whole world seems to know about it."

"Ted was complaining about Lucas being on the panel from the first night we got here," Maura said. "And now that Lucas has been replaced by Grace Hammel, I'm sure Ted's doubly pleased."

"Why?" Nancy asked, her pulse quickening. "What's Ted's connection to Grace Hammel?"

"She's a good friend of Ted's teacher," Maura said. "It's an incredibly lucky break."

"His teacher taught at Grace Hammel's music school for a couple of years before she went out on her own," Abby explained.

"Of course one judge doesn't decide who wins," Maura added. "But a judge with a strong opinion can influence the other judges."

"How many judges are there?" Nancy asked.

"Three," Maura said. "Why are you so interested?"

Nancy shrugged. "I was looking forward to seeing Lucas in action, and I'm sorry he dropped out of the judging," she said cautiously. "I thought you might know the real reason he left." Noting Maura's puzzled expression, she added quickly, "I mean, what his other commitments might be."

"I have no idea. I haven't heard anything about it at all," Maura replied. "Have you, Abby?" she asked, turning to her friend.

Abby shook her head. "Not a word, I'm afraid."

"Well, like I said, everyone's sorry about it, except for Ted," Maura said.

Nancy nodded thoughtfully. The four of them left the hotel together, then parted company when they reached the street.

"See you around," Maura said as she got into her car with Abby.

Nancy smiled and waved. "Count on it," she said under her breath.

"What did you make of that?" Bess asked as they walked back to their own car.

"It seems Ted had a problem with Lucas a couple of years ago," Nancy said thoughtfully. "Of course I'd guess he's over it by now. Maura sure sounded bitter, though."

"And what about Grace Hammel?" Bess asked. "Could Ted have known she'd replace Curt Lucas, and done something to make sure it happened?"

"I don't know," Nancy admitted. "But just knowing a judge doesn't mean you'll win."

"That's true," Bess said. "I just wonder how much of a coincidence it is that someone who knows Ted so well was selected to be a judge."

Nancy started the car. "It's definitely something to think about," she said as they headed for the main road and drove back toward the festival.

"Definitely," Bess said. She paused, then said, "Maura stays at the dorm. Maybe I can catch her later tonight after dinner."

"Good idea," Nancy said, "and I'll talk to Jean-Claude." She drove along the shady road silently for a while, thinking about Maura's attitude toward Ted. Maura was so bitter about being a semifinalist that it seemed more and more likely she might be behind everything. By successfully eliminating at least one finalist, she'd have a good shot at being chosen as the replacement, Nancy reasoned.

Nancy suddenly realized that she should find out who was first on the list of semifinalists, Maura or Jean-Claude. That person would become an even likelier suspect.

"If Maura had food poisoning last year in Cambridge, do you think it might have given her the idea to try it on someone else?" she asked Bess.

Bess thought. "I really don't know. If the same people from this year's contest were with her in Cambridge, doesn't it seem possible that someone here could have been the one who poisoned her there?"

Nancy nodded. "But why would someone have poisoned her in Cambridge? That's what

I can't figure out. She was only a semifinalist, so no one had anything to gain by eliminating her."

Or did they? It suddenly occurred to Nancy that if Maura was first in a line of semifinalists, the person in line behind her might have wanted her out of the way, although a finalist would have been a more obvious choice. She'd have to look into this, too, she decided. It made her uncomfortable to think that Ted might be involved in this somehow. The only person Nancy was counting out was Keiko, since she'd left the festival by the time Maura had been poisoned.

Nancy sighed. "The more I think about the possibilities, the more confusing everything gets."

"I agree," Bess said. "Let's give it a rest for a while, go find our room at the dorm, and relax. Deal?"

"Deal," Nancy said, smiling.

Nancy and Bess reached the dorm at six o'clock. Nancy suggested they find Ted to ask him about their room, but he was nowhere around.

"That's funny. I wonder where he is," she said worriedly. "I hope he had that cut looked at."

"He's probably having dinner somewhere,"

Bess said. "Don't worry, I'm sure we'll run into him later. Why don't we try to find the dorm supervisor instead."

Nancy nodded distractedly. "I wonder if Ted's room has been cleaned up yet," she said. "Let's go check."

They walked down the corridor, passing the dorm kitchen on the way. Nancy was surprised to see Alexander, making himself a cup of tea. She poked her head into the small galleylike space.

"Hello, Alexander," she said. "How are you?"

"I am fine now, thank you," he said stiffly.

"I'm so glad to see you out of the hospital," Nancy continued. "Are you feeling well enough to perform?"

"Of course," he answered vehemently. "No one will keep me from playing on Monday. My rehearsal with the orchestra went well. There were no problems." He stared at Nancy, his chin up, as if challenging her to say something negative.

Nancy could see the mood he was in, and backed out of the small room.

"I'm so glad," she said politely. "We can't wait to hear you play. See you later."

"Whew!" Bess exclaimed as they walked down the hall. "He came back angry."

Nancy nodded. "Not angry, just defensive,"

she said thoughtfully. "I wonder if he knows about the other attacks. He might not feel that he was being singled out if he did." She paused. "You know the kitchen is on the first floor, so it would have been easy for anyone to get to Alexander's mushroom salad without being seen."

Nancy and Bess found the dorm supervisor's room a few doors down from the kitchen. He showed them to the double room he had set aside for them on the first floor, near the pianists.

"Not bad," Bess said as they unpacked their bags and hung up their clothes. She opened the window and looked out. They had a view of the Great Lawn and the orchestra shell. People were already starting to arrive for the evening concert.

"I'm going to love staying here," Bess said, turning away from the window. "It has so much atmosphere."

"I know what you mean," Nancy said. "Everyone is so involved with the music—the people who play here and the people who come to listen. It's as if music were the most important thing in the world."

"No, it's more than that," Bess said. "It's as if music were the *only* thing in the world."

They finished unpacking and changed into light summer dresses for their dinner with

Mrs. Wheeler. Nancy put on a cream-colored sleeveless silk dress and navy sandals. Bess chose a pale blue floral print with low white heels. Then they took a walk around their wing of the dorm. The rooms were labeled with nameplates, which made it easy to find out where each pianist was staying. Their room was next door to Maura's. The two large bathrooms for men and women, each with private shower stalls, were at opposite ends of the hall.

Nancy suggested they check the security office to see if the chief of security was around. They found a tall, lanky man of about thirty-five with short dark hair and dark eyes in the office. He was wearing a uniform, and the plaque on his desk read John Spencer, Chief of Security. Nancy introduced herself and Bess.

"Glad to meet you," he said. "It's not every day we have an incident like the one that happened to Ted Martinelli. I'm glad we had a trained eye on the scene when it happened."

"Have you managed to check the metronome for fingerprints?" Nancy asked.

"Yes, we sent it over to the police lab right away, and apparently there were no prints at all," he said. "We did find out who it belongs to, though," he added.

"Who?" Nancy asked excitedly.

"It belongs to Maura MacDonald."

"Where does she keep it?" Nancy asked.

"On the piano in the common room," he replied.

"I see," Nancy said, disappointed. In that case, anyone could have had access to it.

"Thanks for filling out such a thorough report, by the way," he added, looking at Nancy with interest. "Do you have any ideas about who might have done this?"

"Not really," Nancy said. "But I'll certainly come talk to you if I find out anything more."

"I'd appreciate that," the chief said.

On their way out, they stopped at the reception desk and picked up a schedule for the following week's concerts and the final day of the piano competition, Monday. Nancy looked at her watch.

"We'd better go," she said to Bess as they left the office. "It's almost seven, and we're due at the Dandelion Inn at seven-thirty."

The old coaching inn was the most impressive building in Westbridge, located on Main Street. Nancy and Bess arrived a bit early, ahead of Mrs. Wheeler. The maitre d' escorted them to a table in the main dining room.

"This is gorgeous!" Bess said, eyeing the snowy white linen and crystal chandeliers.

Nancy nodded. "It really is unusual," she said, glancing around. The room was furnished in authentic eighteenth-century style, and the result was elegant and charming. Oak beams lined the ceiling, and the huge open fireplace had a large cast-iron kettle hung from a hook. The floor was carpeted with a richly colored antique rug that glowed in the soft candlelight. The walls were decorated with sepia-tone photographs of the original town of Westbridge. A string quartet played softly in a corner of the room.

Just as they were about to order some soft drinks, Mrs. Wheeler arrived, wearing a black silk dress with a single strand of pearls. She sat down and said breathlessly, "I'm so sorry I'm late, girls. I was waiting for an old friend to show up, and he was delayed. He's just parking the car now."

Nancy acted surprised. "I didn't know someone else was joining us," she said.

"Oh, you'll like him," Mrs. Wheeler said. "He's one of the original festival people, and he's been here for years and years. In fact, he may be able to answer some of your questions about the pianists you're interested in." She picked up her menu, then glancing over Nancy's shoulder, smiled. "Here he is now."

Nancy turned. A tall man with silver hair and familiar chiseled features was approaching, a smile on his face. It was Curt Lucas.

# Chapter Ten

"Hello, everyone. Sorry to be late," Curt Lucas said as he took the seat next to Nancy. He was wearing a black dinner jacket with a maroon vest over a gleaming white shirt. With his silver hair and handsome face, he looked like a Victorian English gentleman.

Mrs. Wheeler introduced them, and when Lucas took a good look at Nancy, he smiled. "I've already met you, riding at Chapin's Horse Farm." Turning to Bess, he added, "And you were in the office with Keiko."

Bess nodded. "I'm surprised you remember. You were only there for a few minutes."

"Yes, but I never forget a pretty face," Lucas said, then laughed, putting Bess at ease.

"I understand that Keiko's wrist has completely healed," Lucas said. "What a relief. Otherwise, it would have meant substituting one of the semifinalists, which would have been a logistical nightmare at this late stage."

"How would a semifinalist have been chosen?" Nancy asked curiously. "I mean, there are two of them."

"Oh, that's easy. All the pianists were given place numbers after the semifinals, according to how their performances were judged. Maura MacDonald was just behind Alexander Poliakin on the list, so she would be the one to replace anyone who had to drop out."

Nancy quickly looked at Bess. They had the answer to their question: Maura had more of a motive to eliminate a finalist than Jean-Claude did.

Then Nancy had another thought: What if Jean-Claude wanted to eliminate Maura in order to move up one position himself? Maybe that was his intention when he hit them with his sailboat.

Just then their waiter arrived to take their orders. Nancy chose the fisherman's stew, a combination of mussels, clams, shrimp, and bluefish in a creamy tomato sauce. Bess couldn't resist the pasta primavera, made with locally grown baby vegetables. The other two both decided on the house specialty: lobster soufflé, served with a delicate lemon sauce.

"When did you start judging the piano competition?" Nancy asked Lucas.

"Oh, many years ago. I'm much older than I look, you know," the composer said with a twinkle in his eye.

"I'm so sorry you won't be judging this year," she said. "I was looking forward to hearing your comments on the performances. I do hope everything is okay," she said tentatively.

"Yes, well, that will have to wait till some other time, unfortunately," Lucas said vaguely. He seemed edgy, and Nancy wondered why. What had made the composer take himself off the panel—or have to leave the panel?

"How do the judges usually get along?" Bess asked. "Do you always agree?"

Lucas didn't respond right away. He drank some of his water, then called the waiter over for more rolls and butter.

Finally he said, "The judges usually manage to find some common ground, but there have been times when . . ." He stopped and carefully chose a whole wheat roll, then cut it neatly in half.

"Anyway," he continued briskly, "let's not talk about me. Tell me about yourselves. What brings you to Westbridge?" he asked. "Are you music lovers?"

"We're on vacation," Nancy said, "and Mrs.

Wheeler was nice enough to let us stay with her while we're here. And I do love music," she added.

"Me, too!" Bess said enthusiastically. "The orchestra rehearsals are wonderful. I've learned so much!"

Lucas smiled. "Yes, that's the great thing about the Muscatonic Festival. You can eat outside, rest in a beautiful setting, and hear one of the world's great orchestras play all at the same time."

"Nancy's father is an old friend of mine," Mrs. Wheeler said. "You remember, I told you about Carson Drew, the lawyer who took care of that legal problem I had."

"Ah, yes." Lucas nodded.

"And Nancy has an extremely unusual talent. She's a successful detective and has solved many mysteries," Mrs. Wheeler said, smiling proudly at Nancy.

Lucas gave Nancy an appraising look. "How interesting," he said. "I never would have guessed it. You look so . . ." He stopped, apparently at a loss for words.

"Normal?" Bess asked with a laugh.

"Yes, I guess so," Lucas said. "Why do you do it?"

Nancy looked at him evenly. "I guess I do it because I like to solve puzzles and help people at the same time."

"Nancy has been approached by two of the pianists to help them find out who's responsible for the attacks being made," Mrs. Wheeler continued.

"You mean there's been more than one attack?" Lucas asked. "I didn't know that. I hope no one has been seriously hurt."

"Not yet," Nancy said, "but it's not for lack of trying. Alexander got food poisoning right after Keiko fell off her horse, and the next day Ted's concerto score was stolen and he was attacked."

"I hadn't heard. This is shocking. I guess I've been too wrapped up in my own problems." He paused thoughtfully, then said, "Could any of these attacks have been accidental? Perhaps Alexander's food poisoning wasn't deliberate."

Nancy explained about Alexander's knowledge of mushrooms, careful to add that the doctor had seemed sure that Alexander could have made a mistake. She wanted to present a full picture. She also explained that Ted's accident had been the most clear-cut attack of all. She was uncomfortable discussing her thoughts in detail because she didn't have all the information she needed to decide what was really going on and who was responsible. Instead, she talked about Keiko's recovery and what a fine pianist she seemed to be.

"Yes, she is wonderful, especially on that Beethoven piano concerto," Lucas said. "Now that I'm not judging, I am free to discuss the finalists."

Nancy suddenly decided to take advantage of this opening and ask Lucas the question she had been dying to ask all through dinner. Taking a deep breath, she asked, "Why did you have to withdraw from the panel this year?"

To Nancy's intense disappointment, Lucas mumbled something about unavoidable circumstances, the same general reason she had heard before. Why won't he talk about it? she wondered. Perhaps it's just too personal. But in the back of her mind, a tiny doubt gnawed at her. She knew that sooner or later, she would have to ask either Lucas or Ted about their disagreement two years earlier.

Just then their dinners arrived and Lucas changed the subject. They discussed different coffees from around the world. But beneath his relaxed exterior, Nancy could detect a deep uneasiness. This was not the man she had heard so much about over the years, the self-assured Broadway composer and award winner. This was a man with a problem.

After dinner Mrs. Wheeler suggested they return to the festival for the final piece of music, which she insisted they could just make if they hustled. As they settled themselves onto a hill near the festival's small lake, the first notes of the *1812* Overture by Tchaikovsky, complete with the sound of cannons and fireworks, were begun.

Nancy was sitting next to Lucas, and he leaned over and asked in a low voice, "Can I trust you?"

Nancy was surprised, but nodded yes. "Of course you can," she said.

"I was impressed with what you said about being a detective, and I have an answer to the question you asked me earlier." He hesitated, searching for the right words. "The real reason for my withdrawal from the panel has nothing to do with conflicting responsibilities. I have withdrawn from the judging because I am being blackmailed."

# Chapter Eleven

NANCY WAS SHOCKED and didn't speak for several moments. Finally she said, "Do you want to talk about this?"

Lucas turned to her. His expression was strained. "Yes," he said slowly. "Could we go somewhere less crowded and less noisy."

Nancy agreed, and they got up and walked away from the crowd on the hill, back toward the practice rooms.

The building was dark except for a glimmer of light coming through the basement windows. Lucas guided Nancy through the maze of hallways downstairs to a large room with a beautiful mahogany grand piano. The room was unusual because it also had a sofa, two chairs, and a coffee table. Lucas gestured for Nancy to sit.

"I use this room a lot because I can have conferences in here," Lucas explained. "The piano happens to be one of the best in the building." He sat at the keyboard. "And I keep my scores here," he said, gesturing to indicate a small cabinet in the corner.

"I guess I'd better tell you everything that's happened," he said. "It all began a few weeks before the competition was scheduled to start. My studio was broken into, and a valuable score was stolen."

Nancy drew in her breath sharply. "That's the same thing that happened to Ted," she murmured.

"Not exactly," Lucas said. "On the first day of the competition, a photocopy of the score arrived in the mail with a threatening note attached."

Lucas walked to the cabinet, unlocked it, and took out a manila folder. Inside was the copy of the score and the note. He handed both to Nancy. The note read, "Step down or I go public with this." It was composed of letters cut from a newspaper and glued together.

Nancy looked at the score. It had no title. "Would you play this for me?" she asked.

"Of course," Lucas said. He played a series of short tunes that didn't seem connected in any way, and yet they sounded vaguely familiar to Nancy.

"What is this music from?" Nancy asked. "Why is it so valuable?"

Lucas sighed. "These tunes are actually three separate themes composed by my old teacher, Alfred Cole. Have you ever heard of him?"

"I think so," Nancy said. "Didn't he write Broadway musicals in the thirties?"

"That's him," Lucas said, nodding. "He was one of the greatest, right up there with the Gershwins and Cole Porter. Before he died, he gave the themes to me as a legacy. He wanted me to use them because he knew he never would."

"What's the difference between a theme and a song?" Nancy asked, confused.

"Well, a theme is a single melody to be used in different ways throughout a song. Every song has a theme, and variations of the theme make up the song. A good theme is important to any piece of music. You could say it's the heart of the music, I guess."

Lucas stopped and gazed at the score again. He shook his head. "Who would have believed such a generous gift could have caused so much trouble."

"Why?" Nancy asked. "What happened?"

"I was writing my first musical," Lucas

began. "Alfred knew this, and that was when he gave me his themes. The three songs I wrote from them made me famous. That's probably why the themes sound familiar to you—those songs have been performed a lot over the years."

Nancy nodded. "Go on," she said encouragingly.

"Anyway, I never told anyone that the themes were written by someone else. By the time the musical was performed, Alfred was dead, and I was afraid my sudden success would vanish, so I simply kept my mouth shut about the themes."

"Do you feel that your reputation would be ruined now if people found out Cole wrote the themes?" Nancy asked. "You actually wrote the finished songs yourself. Isn't that what matters?"

Lucas sighed. "No, that isn't the only thing that matters," he said. "Many would feel it's plagiarism," he said.

"I don't think so," Nancy said. "Plagiarism is stealing someone else's work and taking credit for it. Cole *gave* you those themes."

Lucas nodded. "That's true. But I did not give Cole credit as the cocreator of the work. Plagiarism is a very dirty word in the music business, the same as in the publishing world," he said. "If it were to come out that I didn't credit the cocreator, there would be a lot of trouble. Bad publicity doesn't even begin to describe it. There might even be lawsuits from Cole's music publishers. Who knows?

"The point is, I was young and stupid. I should have done something about this years ago, but I kept putting it off, out of fear or vanity or both. And now it's too late. I would be ruined." Lucas's voice had become progressively lower, until Nancy had to strain to hear him.

What a mess! she thought. And now someone is blackmailing him over this.

"What proof does the blackmailer have that the themes were written by Alfred Cole?" she asked.

Lucas handed Nancy the score. It was covered with tiny, scribbled notes, which were barely readable.

"These notes are in Alfred's handwriting, and any music scholar would know the handwriting," Lucas explained. "Often, a great composer's original scores are photographed and made available to historians and other musicians. People have been looking at Alfred's handwriting in music archives for years.

"There's something else," he continued.

"The blackmailer also stole a letter I received from Cole, dedicating the themes to me. It proved without a doubt that he intended me to use his music. With the letter, I might have stood a chance if the truth were to come out. Without it, I had no choice but to withdraw from the panel," he finished grimly.

Nancy sat quietly for a while, absorbing everything Lucas had said. Finally she asked, "Who knows that you keep important papers here instead of in your apartment in New York City?"

"Oh, everyone, I guess," Lucas said, frowning. "This has been my preferred residence for many years. And I don't even bother to lock my door half the time. Why should I? It's usually so quiet around here, and for the most part, musicians don't tend to be thieves." He smiled sadly. "I got a new lock for my cabinet the day after this happened."

Just then Nancy heard a sound outside the practice room. Putting her finger to her lips, she got up and tiptoed to the door. Nancy heard a slight scratching sound, almost like that of a match being lit.

Nancy threw open the door. Standing there was a woman in her midforties with sharp features, shoulder-length dark hair, and glasses.

Lucas stood behind Nancy. "You might as well join us," he said to the woman in a grim voice. "Nancy, meet Grace Hammel, the musician who will be replacing me on the panel."

# Chapter Twelve

NANCY WOULD ALWAYS REMEMBER the expression on Grace Hammel's face. It was a combination of surprise, defensiveness, and bad temper. She took a step backward as if expecting Nancy to hit her.

"I guess you felt like getting in a little late practice?" Lucas asked sarcastically.

"As a matter of fact, I do like to practice late. There aren't many people around, and I have the place to myself, more or less." Grace made no move to step inside the practice room.

"Oh, stop lurking and come in, Grace," Lucas said impatiently, gesturing for her to enter.

Hammel seemed to relax a bit. "I felt as if I'd interrupted an important conversation," she explained, walking into the room. "And since I don't like it when people do that to me, I thought you would probably be angry."

"Not at all, not at all," Lucas said heartily. Nancy couldn't interpret his tone of voice. Either he was genuinely pleased to see Grace Hammel, or he was doing a good job of acting.

Grace sat down on the piano bench. Lucas frowned, clearly feeling displaced, and sat in one of the armchairs. Nancy perched on the sofa.

"What can you tell me about the finalists, Curt?" Hammel asked. "I'm coming into the game at a late stage, and information would help."

"Let me see," Curt began. "Well, I'll tell you one thing that I've just learned. They've all been the victims of a series of pranks, pretty serious ones. The Yamamoto girl fell from her horse and sprained her wrist, and Poliakin had food poisoning. Apparently, Ted Martinelli, whom I understand you know quite well, had his notated concerto score stolen and was attacked in his room."

Grace stared at Lucas. "Why didn't anyone tell me about all this?" she asked. "Will they be able to perform on Monday?"

Nancy couldn't tell whether or not her surprise was genuine. Surely someone would have told Grace on her arrival, she thought.

"Tell me about their playing last week. How did they do in the solo performances?" Grace asked.

"Quite well, really," Lucas replied. "All of them chose difficult pieces, especially Poliakin, who went for Schumann's *Carnival.* Oh, yes, this year Schumann is the favorite. We've had quite a lot of him."

"I've never liked *Carnival,"* Grace said. "It's probably a good thing I missed that."

"Yes, well, you won't miss Martinelli's performance of the Schumann concerto."

Grace's expression brightened. "Did he choose that in the end? I'm glad—he plays it so well."

"Hmm," Lucas replied. His expression showed no emotion. He obviously didn't want to be drawn into a conversation about Ted Martinelli and so changed the topic.

"Keiko Yamamoto will be playing the *Emperor* Concerto, you know," he said.

"How brave of her!" Grace exclaimed.

"Why is that?" Nancy asked curiously. This discussion of different pieces of music, and what they implied about the pianist who chose them, was new to her.

"Beethoven's fifth piano concerto, known as the *Emperor,* is one of the most difficult pieces in the repertory. It takes great concentration, great technical skill, and above all great 'soul.'" Lucas looked at Grace for confirmation, and she nodded.

"Wait till you hear it," she said to Nancy. "If it's played well, it's one of the most beautiful and exhilarating pieces of music ever written."

She turned to Lucas. "Do you think Yamamoto has it in her?" she asked.

Lucas shrugged. "Maybe," he said. "If her wrist doesn't act up, and if she can clean up one or two sloppy passages, I think she'll be fine."

Suddenly Grace turned to Nancy. "How rude of me. Here we are, chattering away about the finalists, and I don't even know your name."

Before she could answer, Lucas said, "This is Nancy Drew. She's the daughter of a friend of Myrna Wheeler, and she's here because she loves music. We were just talking about the piano, which is her favorite instrument." Staring hard at Nancy, he said, "Isn't that right?"

Nancy nodded. "That about covers it," she said. Lucas had just skillfully glossed over the real reason for their talk. Of course, he wouldn't want Grace to know what they'd been talking about, or even to know that Nancy was a detective.

Lucas stood up and stretched. "We should really be going," he said to Nancy, raising an eyebrow slightly. "We left our companions back on the hillside.

"This piano is a good one, by the way," he added. "A rebuilt Steinway. I think you'll appreciate the tone."

Grace nodded. "Well, good luck, Curt. Sorry to meet again under these circumstances." She quickly bit her lip, as if realizing that she'd said something awkward.

"What circumstances?" Lucas said. "You'll do a great job, I'm sure, and I'll be busy elsewhere."

As they walked back toward the lake, Nancy saw a sudden burst of bright red, white, and blue light and watched it fade slowly in the sky. "I guess that's the end of the fireworks," she said.

Lucas nodded. "I'm sorry you missed them."

Nancy was quiet for a moment, trying to think of a way to broach the question that was on her mind. She decided to be direct. "What do you think of Ted Martinelli?" she asked.

Lucas took his time answering. "I think he's a well-trained pianist," he finally answered. His voice lacked enthusiasm.

"It sounds as if you don't think much of his playing," Nancy persisted.

"No, it's not that. He's a perfectly adequate pianist, and he's obviously absorbed everything his teachers had to offer."

Nancy thought that the word *adequate* had never sounded quite so damaging.

"To put it another way," Lucas continued, "I feel that his playing lacks heart. But that's just my opinion. Others disagree."

Nancy knew exactly what he meant by "heart," because of Keiko's explanation of musicianship. It seemed clear to Nancy that Curt simply didn't like the way Ted played the piano.

"What about the other two finalists?" Nancy asked. "What are their qualities?"

"Oh, I think they're both very sound in their own ways," Lucas said. "Keiko Yamamoto has a beautifully expressive tone, and the Poliakin boy has strength. His fingers are like steel."

The image of steel-like hands smashing the metronome down on Ted's head came into Nancy's mind. She pushed it away and asked, "What about the semifinalists?"

"Yes, they're both good, and I imagine they'll get there someday if they have the desire and the patience to persevere," Lucas said.

Nancy decided to tackle the subject uppermost in Curt's mind. "Do you have any idea about who might be blackmailing you?" she asked, watching his face carefully.

Lucas took an old wooden pipe out of his pocket. He stuck it in the corner of his mouth and drew hard on it. Noticing Nancy's puzzled expression, he smiled. "No, there's no tobacco in it. I had to give up smoking. I just use this as a sort of prop. I find it comforting." He chewed thoughtfully on the pipe, then said, "No, I have no idea who might be blackmailing me. It's such a vindictive thing to do. I've always thought of myself as a likable person."

Nancy wondered if he was leaving out any information and decided to prod a bit. "This competition is extremely important, with huge rewards for the winning pianist. It could actually mean the difference between having a good career and no career at all. What if one of the finalists felt you would stand in the way of winning?"

"I know what you're getting at, but I just don't believe any of these finalists could be that desperate. They're all in top form, they're all young, and I imagine that all of them will be successful without my help."

Yes, Nancy thought, but what if one of them isn't willing to wait? She could see that Lucas was unwilling to say that one of the finalists was blackmailing him, but it seemed to her that it was an obvious conclusion. Who else would have such a clear motive to get him out of the way?

Suddenly the image of Grace Hammel came to her. Perhaps there was someone else with a good motive. Nancy made a mental note to check out Grace as soon as possible.

"Do you think a semifinalist might feel bitter enough to sabotage the finalists?" she asked.

"No, I don't think so. They all know the odds when they start. You're a semifinalist for a while, and then, if you're any good, you become a finalist. And with any luck, one day you win. They all know about this process. Everyone goes through it. Being a semifinalist is an honor, you know. They're chosen from hundreds of other competitors."

On returning to the hillside, they found Bess and Mrs. Wheeler still sitting comfortably side by side, talking quietly.

"Nan," Bess said. "Where have you been?" She looked at Lucas, who had sat down beside Mrs. Wheeler, then back at Nancy, raising her eyebrows questioningly.

"I'll tell you about it later," Nancy said under her breath.

"Well, you missed Ted," Bess said. "He

invited us to come with him to a local rock club, where some of the festival musicians go to jam after hours."

"That sounds great," Nancy said. Looking around, she asked, "Where is he? Did he tell you how to get there, or are we supposed to go with him?"

"He just went back to the dorm to get his jacket and helmet," Bess said. "I told him we'd meet him in the parking lot as soon as you showed up."

Nancy said good night to Mrs. Wheeler and thanked her for the wonderful dinner. "And thank you, too," she told Lucas. "I was most intrigued by our conversation. I hope we'll be in touch soon," she said mysteriously, in case anyone was listening in. Lucas took her hand and thanked her for all her help.

"What was that all about?" Bess asked curiously as they walked to the parking lot.

Nancy filled her in on her talk with Lucas. They discussed Grace Hammel, and Bess agreed that there might be a hidden motive for blackmail lurking behind that friendly exterior.

Uneasily, Nancy admitted that she was also concerned about Ted's possible motive for wanting Lucas out of the way. "How can you find out more without being obvious?" Bess asked.

"I don't know, but I'll think of something," Nancy said. "Anyway, we can probably find out what we need to know about Grace Hammel by talking to Ted."

Ted was waiting for them in the parking lot, leaning against his motorcycle.

"Nancy!" he exclaimed, straightening up as he saw them approaching. "I'm glad you could make it. You are coming, aren't you?" he asked.

"Definitely," Nancy said. She could see a small white bandage on the side of his head where he had been hit. "How is that cut healing?" she asked.

"Oh, it's all right," he said. "Anyway, my headache's gone, thank goodness."

"We stopped by to see you earlier, but you were out," she explained.

"That must have been around dinnertime," Ted replied. "I went to the cafeteria to get a bite to eat. I slept for a couple of hours, and I was starving when I woke up. I guess that's a good sign, right?"

"Right," Nancy said, smiling. "Now, what about this rock club?"

"I really think you'll like it," Ted said enthusiastically. "Oh, Bess, Jean-Claude mentioned to me that he'd be there."

Bess smiled. "Great," she said.

Ted took a piece of folded paper from his

back pocket and gave it to Nancy. "These are the directions," he said. "It's really very easy. It's called the Last Chance Supper Club, and it's only about a twenty-minute drive from here."

"We could follow you," Nancy suggested.

"You could, but I like to ride very fast." He laughed. "It's one of my character flaws."

Nancy studied the piece of paper. "Okay," she said. "We'll meet you there."

Ted strapped on his helmet. "I'm off!" He got on his bike and roared out of the parking lot.

As Nancy and Bess got into the convertible, Nancy handed Bess the directions. "I hope you don't mind navigating," she said. "You can use the light over the vanity mirror if you need to."

Bess switched on the tiny light and read through the directions as Nancy pulled out of the lot. "Take your first left off Westbridge Road and drive for five miles."

Nancy nodded happily. She enjoyed driving on country roads at night, when the heat of the day had evaporated and the air was cool. The sound of crickets was soothing, as were the dark shadows of trees arching high overhead.

The road was winding and narrow, empty except for the convertible. Nancy frowned as she concentrated to navigate around a sharp curve.

As she pulled out of the curve, a yellow hazard sign appeared out of the darkness directly in front of her. Nancy turned the wheel sharply to the right to avoid hitting it, and the car swerved off the road.

# Chapter Thirteen

NANCY HIT THE BRAKES, and the car screeched to a stop inches from a ditch at the side of the road.

"Are you all right, Bess?" she asked anxiously. Bess's eyes were wide, and she was gripping Nancy's arm.

"Yes," Bess said, relaxing her grip. "What was that?"

"It was a hazard sign," Nancy said, "but what was it doing in the middle of the road?" She was preparing to pull back onto the road when she saw the glare of headlights approaching from the opposite direction. The car pulled off the road and parked.

Nancy and Bess exchanged a quick glance. "What now?" Nancy asked.

A man got out of the car and walked toward them. Slowly they could make out his face in the headlights: It was Alexander Poliakin.

"Hello," Nancy said as he lowered his head to the window.

"Are you all right?" Alexander asked. "I thought something might be wrong."

"We're all right, thanks," Nancy said, "but we almost had an accident. There's something strange going on. Someone put a hazard sign right in the middle of the road. We almost hit it."

Alexander was puzzled. "I drove down this road in your direction less than an hour ago, and there was no hazard sign. Let's go take a look."

Nancy and Bess got out of the car and walked to the sign with Alexander.

"I think we should move it," Alexander said. "There's nothing dangerous in either direction on this road." He dragged the sign off the road and left it beside a tree.

"What are you doing here, anyway?" Nancy asked. "We haven't passed any other cars."

"I was listening to music at the rock club," Alexander said. "Some of the festival musicians play together with local people. It's a tradition, I guess." He shrugged and glanced at his watch. "I must go," he said. "It's getting late, and I have an early start tomorrow. You're sure you're all right?"

"Yes, we're fine," Nancy said. "See you soon." They watched as Alexander crossed the road to his car and headed back toward the festival. Then Nancy pulled onto the road and continued the drive to the Last Chance Supper Club.

"Did he seem to be acting strange to you?" Bess asked.

"Yes," Nancy said. "He seemed uneasy."

"Could he have put the hazard sign there himself?" Bess wondered aloud. "That was a really weird place for it to be. And he was the only other driver on the road. It seems like a big coincidence."

Nancy nodded thoughtfully. "And you think he might have been waiting down the road to check his handiwork to see if we had an accident?" She was silent for a few minutes. "But what would he have to gain? It only makes sense if he was responsible for all the other incidents. And that would mean he poisoned himself deliberately to mislead us."

"I guess that doesn't really make much sense," Bess said glumly. "He was pretty sick."

"Yes, he was," Nancy admitted. "I guess it's possible that the hazard sign was actually put there for a reason. We could check on Monday with the roads department."

Nancy wasn't satisfied with their theory about Alexander. Something felt wrong. If Alexander knew a lot about mushrooms, perhaps he could have eaten just enough of the salad to make himself appear very sick. And he could have sabotaged Keiko's horse and hit Ted over the head and stolen his score. Lucas's image of fingers of steel lingered uneasily in her mind.

She suddenly wondered if there could be a connection between the incidents involving the finalists and the blackmail of Curt Lucas. If everything was being engineered by the same person, the motive would have to be very strong.

A tiny, nagging voice in Nancy's head kept bothering her. It was whispering Ted's name, and it had nothing to do with romance. It had to do with ambition and impatience.

"Bess," she said hesitantly, "what about Ted? We know he took this road to the club. He could have put the road sign there, couldn't he?"

Bess acted surprised. "Do you really think Ted could have done this? How would he have carried that big sign and stand on his motorbike?"

"I suppose it's not very likely," Nancy agreed. "Though he's still one of the suspects, no matter how much I wish he weren't," she said, casting a sidelong glance at Bess.

Bess grinned. "I know, just like Jean-Claude. Well, let's hope that neither of them is guilty. Maybe it's none of the people we know," she added hopefully.

Nancy smiled, but in her heart she knew it had to be one of the pianists or Grace Hammel. Otherwise, none of the incidents made sense.

Following Ted's directions, they soon arrived at the Last Chance and pulled into the crowded parking area. Nancy spotted Ted right away. He was standing near the door, talking to some musicians holding guitar cases. When he saw them, he came over to join them.

"What happened to you?" he asked. "I thought you'd be here ages ago. Even if you were driving slowly, it shouldn't have taken you this long. Did you get lost?"

Nancy explained what had happened. Ted seemed mystified. "I didn't see any sign on that road."

"Why was it so deserted?" Nancy asked him. "There was almost no one else on the road. Is there another way to get here?"

"Yes, there is," Ted said, "but I like finding shortcuts. I've been using that back road a lot, and I've told only a few people about it."

Grinning sheepishly, he explained, "It's really fun to drive it on the bike. I can race, and there's never much traffic. But I'm really sorry you had that trouble."

Taking Nancy's arm, he escorted the girls into the club. The room was dark, and a rock band was playing on the stage. There were people everywhere, sitting at small round tables and standing in clusters. The noise level was high, but the acoustics were good, and Nancy could hear conversations nearby. Nancy spotted Keiko and Maura MacDonald sitting together at a table just as Ted asked her to dance.

Nancy said, "I'd love to." Turning to Bess, she said in a low voice, "Now is a perfect chance to talk to Maura. She's probably more relaxed here than at the festival." Bess nodded and headed for Maura's table.

Ted turned out to be a wonderful dancer. He and Nancy moved together as if they'd rehearsed every step. They moved easily into each other's arms as the band shifted into a slow song. Ted put his arms around Nancy's waist and whispered into her ear, "This feels right." He started to hum softly.

Nancy nodded, her cheek pressed against Ted's. She had to admit, it felt wonderful to be in his arms. What was happening to her? As the mood of the music became slower and more hypnotic, Ted held her closer. He moved his head back slightly and looked at her seriously for a long moment, his green eyes searching her face. Then he kissed her lightly on the lips.

Nancy was taken by surprise. She hadn't expected this to happen—and she hadn't expected to feel this way. When the music ended, she and Ted stared at each other for several moments. Then Nancy said breathlessly, "I could really use a soda." Ted nodded and they walked back to the table where Bess was sitting with Keiko and Maura.

Ted offered to get sodas. As he threaded his way through the crowd, Nancy caught sight of Grace Hammel sitting in a dark corner. She was talking to a man, but Nancy couldn't see who it was. She was curious and waited for the crowd to shift so she could see his face.

Suddenly the man standing in front of Grace's table moved to the left, giving Nancy a clear view of Grace's companion. Nancy was shocked to see that it was Alexander Poliakin. He and Grace had their heads close together, and they seemed to be having an intimate conversation. Nancy's mind began to race. Why had Alexander pretended to be returning to the festival? What was he hiding?

# Chapter Fourteen

NANCY DECIDED to move closer to Grace and Alexander's table. Slowly she maneuvered through the room, keeping out of their line of vision as much as possible. Their table was near the ladies' room, where there was a long line of girls. By standing in line, she was able to come within a few feet of the pair without being noticed.

She could barely make out what they were saying over the loud music. Bits and pieces came to her, individual words and phrases. They seemed to be talking about Curt Lucas, because Nancy heard his name mentioned several times.

Finally the musicians took a break, and Grace's voice was suddenly audible. Nancy heard her say, "I always liked that expression, 'You scratch my back, I'll scratch yours.' This is why being a judge comes in handy."

Nancy couldn't believe her ears. Was Grace Hammel actually making some kind of deal with Alexander about awarding him first prize? What other exchange could she be talking about? Whatever it was, Nancy didn't like the sound of it.

Nancy was dying to hear Alexander's response, but the band chose that moment to start up again. Frustrated, she stayed in her position near the ladies' room for a while, but it became impossible for her to hear anything but the loud music. She finally gave up and made her way back to the table.

When she returned, Ted was still off getting their drinks and Bess was looking around wistfully. "I thought Jean-Claude was supposed to be here. Have you seen him?" she asked.

"No, I haven't," Nancy said, "but listen to what I just heard." Checking to make sure Maura and Keiko couldn't hear, she filled Bess in on the bits of conversation she had picked up.

"Wow!" Bess said. "Does this mean they might be behind Lucas's blackmail?"

"Exactly what I was wondering," Nancy said. "Alexander could have gotten hold of

Alfred Cole's score and letter and given them to Grace. She could then have blackmailed Lucas into dropping out."

"How would she have known she would get the job if Lucas left?" asked Bess.

"The way I understand it, the festival has a backup list of judges in case of emergencies. She would have known she was number one on the list," Nancy explained.

"But what does Grace get out of it if she gives first prize to Alexander?" Bess wondered.

"That's the question, isn't it?" Nancy replied. "It must have something to do with her music school. Maybe Alexander has promised to become a teacher there if he wins, which would be a major draw for piano students. Or maybe he's promised to get her involved in some of the contracts that are always offered to the winner, like recording deals, product endorsements, concert dates—there's so much money involved."

Bess's eyes grew large. "This sounds more and more like the explanation, doesn't it?" she said.

"Yes, except for one nagging fact. Alexander really was poisoned by wild mushrooms. Would he have taken so big a risk just to draw suspicion away from himself?" Nancy asked.

Bess sighed. "I don't know," she said. "It seems unlikely, but all the other pieces fit."

Nancy nodded. "Also, if we assume that one of the accidents was staged, it was the easiest one to accomplish. Keiko couldn't have known how badly she'd be hurt by falling from a horse, and Ted couldn't control how badly his head would be hurt. . . ." She stopped in midsentence, her eyes narrowing. She looked speculatively at Bess. Would a head injury be all that hard to fake? she wondered.

Bess said quietly, "I had a chance to question Maura while you were gone. She seems to have an alibi for all of the incidents, including the attack on Ted." When Nancy nodded glumly, Bess added, "But don't dismiss her yet. I think she might be lying about at least one of her alibis. I'll tell you about it later."

This is getting more and more complicated, Nancy thought. So many people seemed to have the motive to eliminate other competitors so they could get ahead. She couldn't completely discount anyone, at least not yet. The only person who still seemed unlikely as a suspect was Keiko, who wasn't there when Maura's food poisoning had occurred.

Suddenly thirsty, Nancy looked for Ted, but the crowds of people made it impossible to locate him. When she turned around again, she saw a glass in front of her on the table.

"Whose soda is this?" she asked Bess. "I didn't notice it before."

Bess said, "I think that must be the one Ted got for you. He couldn't carry everyone's drink at once, so he's making two trips."

Nancy asked Keiko and Maura if the drink belonged to either of them, but they reassured her that it must be hers. She took a sip. It was ginger ale and tasted nice and cold.

Just then Nancy heard Keiko say something that caught her attention.

"Luckily, my wrist is fine, but I'm so afraid now that something else will go wrong. I don't dare practice late at night anymore. It's very frustrating."

Nancy nodded sympathetically. "Do you think someone is still out to hurt you?"

Keiko gazed down at her hands, which were folded on the table. "Yes, I'm afraid of this all the time. There is never a moment when I feel completely free of fear." Nancy hadn't realized how worried the pianist was. Of course, she should have known that it would be impossible for anyone to shrug off the psychological effects of an attack in such a short time. Keiko's usual display of optimism was just that—a display for the benefit of others.

"I'm so sorry, Keiko," Nancy said.

"I'm relieved not to be a target this year. It must be awful for all of you," Maura added.

Maura was certainly acting more relaxed than Nancy had seen her. She realized then that this was a good opportunity to hear what the two pianists thought about Lucas backing out and Grace Hammel replacing him. She decided to introduce the subject as subtly as possible.

"Lucas was very upset when I told him what had happened to your wrist," Nancy said to Keiko.

She nodded. "He was really nice—he offered to get me a specialist if I needed one."

Nancy continued. "It's such a shame that he had to back out. He must be a very busy man."

"It was quite a coincidence," Maura said angrily. "I just found out that Ted's teacher sits on the board of directors for the festival."

So she is still harping on that, Nancy thought. Maura seemed obsessed with the idea that Ted had something to do with Grace Hammel's replacing Lucas. And yet it seemed that Alexander was benefiting from the change in judges, not Ted.

Nancy sighed to herself. So Ted's teacher sat on the board. Did that mean she could have influenced the festival to choose Grace as Lucas's replacement? Maybe, but that didn't mean that Grace would award first prize to Ted automatically.

Did Maura's attitude indicate a grudge against Ted so deep that she might have stolen his score?

Looking across the room, Nancy realized that Ted had been gone for an awfully long time. The crowd was even denser than before, and Ted must have gotten the rest of the sodas by now. She decided to help him carry them.

She got up and made her way across the dark and crowded dance floor toward the soft drink bar. Without warning she felt herself growing faint. The room began to spin, and the music became much louder. Then the noise and light were abruptly cut off for her as if someone had slammed a door. Then Nancy fell to the floor in the middle of the crowd of dancers!

# Chapter Fifteen

LUCKILY the music stopped just as Nancy fell, and the dancers stopped too. Almost as if it were happening to someone else, Nancy felt herself being lifted up in slow motion and carried off the dance floor to a chair at the side of the room.

Nancy thought she could hear Bess's voice, but it sounded muffled, as if it were coming from a long distance away through heavy fog.

"What happened?" Nancy heard Bess ask.

A man's voice responded. "She passed out on the dance floor," he explained.

Nancy's vision slowly cleared, and she could make out Bess and the man who had carried her off the floor. Soon the rest of the room came into focus. "Bess? Is that you?" she murmured groggily.

"Yes, it's me, Nan," Bess said. She took Nancy's hand and squeezed it gently.

"What happened?" Nancy asked, sitting up and looking around. "I was trying to get through that crowd of dancers, and then—"

"And then you must have fainted. How do you feel now?" Bess asked anxiously.

"I'm a little groggy, but okay," Nancy said, shaking her head as if to clear it. "I could use some fresh air."

By now, Maura and Keiko had arrived, and the three of them helped Nancy outside into the cool night air.

"Maybe it was something you ate at dinner," Bess said. "Didn't you have the fisherman's stew?"

"Yes," Nancy said, "I can always tell when seafood is bad, and the stew was very fresh. It had to be something else." She thought for a moment, then said, "There was that drink I just had. Can you go in and get the glass? I don't think I could face that crowd right now."

"I'll get it," Maura volunteered, and ran back inside. She returned empty-handed.

"Sorry," she said, "the table was already cleared, and other people were sitting there. It's a mob scene. No chance of finding it now, I'm afraid."

Nancy couldn't be certain, but it seemed to her that Maura was just a tiny bit relieved about the missing glass. Could she have had something to do with it?

"Maybe we should go in to try to find whoever cleared the table," Nancy said to Bess. She doubted they'd find anything, but it was worth a try.

"If you really want to, I'll do it, Nan," Bess said, "but you don't look so good. I think we should call it a night and go back to the dorm."

"You're probably right," Nancy said reluctantly. She was annoyed at herself for feeling so weak. Under any other circumstances, she would have looked for the missing glass. But she knew she couldn't do it now.

"I guess we'll be going now," she said to Maura and Keiko. "When you see Ted, would you tell him what happened?"

The girls promised to let Ted know. Nancy and Bess made their way across the parking lot toward the convertible, moving slowly because Nancy still felt a bit dizzy. Just as they were getting into the car, Ted appeared.

"Leaving so soon?" he asked, smiling warmly. "The night's still young."

His smile faded as Nancy explained what had happened. "You mean, someone put something in your drink?" he asked, shocked.

"It looks that way," Nancy said.

"Let me come back with you to the dorm," Ted said with concern.

"No, really, I'm all right now. I just want to get to sleep, and Bess can drive the car. I'll see you in the morning."

Ted seemed unconvinced, but he gave in anyway. "Take care of her," he said to Bess. He put his hand on Nancy's arm. "I don't want anything to happen to you. Promise me you'll be careful."

Nancy smiled and told him not to worry. He took her hand in his and lifted it to his lips. "Good night, Nancy," he said. "Sweet dreams."

As he walked back across the parking lot to the club, Bess looked at Nancy.

"Don't say a word," Nancy cautioned her friend. "We're just friends. He's a nice guy."

"And a great dancer," Bess added with a smile.

"And a great dancer," Nancy repeated. "Now, can we please get going?"

"Of course," Bess said as she started up the car.

The drive back to the dorm was uneventful. Nancy noticed that the hazard sign was no longer standing beside the tree where they had put it. Oh, well, just one more thing to check on Monday, she said to herself.

After parking the car in the dorm parking

lot, they made their way to their room. Exhausted, Nancy quickly got ready for bed. Just before she fell asleep, she remembered something. The last thing she had heard before passing out on the dance floor was one of Alfred Cole's themes. She would have to tell Bess about it tomorrow. For now, she couldn't keep her eyes open another minute.

The next morning Nancy woke refreshed and feeling no ill effects. She and Bess went out for Sunday brunch at a local restaurant famous for its waffles and homemade muffins.

After ordering the house special of whole wheat waffles with blueberries, Nancy said, "Bess, I need you to help me piece together what happened last night."

"I'll try," Bess said. "What do you want to know?"

"Well, to begin with, were any of the festival musicians playing just before we left?"

"I think I remember seeing a couple of people on the stage at different times," Bess replied.

"Like who?" Nancy asked, excited.

"Alexander was playing the drums at one point, which was a surprise. Did you know he could play?" Bess asked.

Nancy shook her head. "Who else?"

"Maura and Keiko both took turns playing the piano while you and Ted were dancing," Bess continued, "and again later, when you went off to listen to Grace Hammel."

Nancy was surprised to hear that. "You mean Maura and Keiko both play rock?"

Bess nodded. "You should have heard them—they were both really good, especially Maura. If she doesn't end up with a classical career, she could definitely join a rock band."

"I'm not sure that's what she's after," Nancy said with a wry smile. "Was there anyone else?"

"I can't think of anyone," Bess said. "Ted said that Jean-Claude was supposed to be jamming last night, but I never saw him. Of course, that doesn't mean he wasn't there," she said, the disappointment showing on her face. "Oh, and after you went off to find Ted, I saw him onstage playing a couple of minutes with Maura. Why do you want to know?"

"You mean they sat at the piano together and played at the same time?" Nancy asked.

Bess nodded.

Nancy told Bess what she had remembered just before falling asleep—that someone had played an Alfred Cole theme. She had to know who it was.

"I have a feeling there's a connection, that

whoever was playing last night might be the blackmailer we're looking for. That theme was just one coincidence too many."

Bess nodded excitedly. "Why would someone play a Broadway theme in the middle of a rock set?"

Nancy looked grim. "My thought exactly," she said.

They finished their brunch and returned to the dorm, where they found many musicians in the common room relaxing and chatting.

Nancy couldn't get the idea out of her head that the blackmailer had been at the club the night before, jamming with the other musicians. The image of Maura and Ted playing together refused to go away. One of them had introduced that theme, Nancy thought, but which one? She and Bess found two free chairs, but as soon as Nancy sat down, she jumped up again.

"I can't stand this," she said to Bess in a low voice. "I have to look for that stolen score, and this seems to be a perfect time. A lot of people are out of their rooms."

"But how are you going to get in without keys?" Bess asked.

"All of the rooms on this floor have windows," Nancy said, "and on a day like this, the windows will all be open. It should be easy."

Bess turned to her friend, looking doubtful,

but agreed that it was a good time to do it. "Just be careful," she said."

Nancy squeezed Bess's arm. "Don't worry."

She slipped unobtrusively out of the room and made her way around the side of the building to the courtyard that all of the pianists' rooms faced. Just as she had guessed, all the windows were open.

She remembered that the first room belonged to Maura. Looking around carefully to make sure she was unobserved, she hoisted herself up and over the windowsill.

Maura's room was very neat. The bed was made, and no clothes were lying around. Quickly Nancy went through the drawers in the night table and desk, then opened the suitcase in the closet. She found several musical scores, but they were all pieces that she would expect to find in a pianist's room—music by the great classical composers. There was nothing even slightly suspicious looking, and certainly nothing with handwritten notes on it.

So much for Maura being the culprit, Nancy thought, frustrated. She left the same way she'd come in and then tried each of the other rooms. Within a short time she had checked every suspect's room, including Grace Hammel's, and had found nothing.

Nancy stood in the courtyard, thinking

hard. What would be the safest place to hide a piece of music, where no one would think twice about seeing it? It suddenly struck her that there was one other area she should be checking—the practice rooms. Several of the pianists kept their sheet music there. Why not a stolen score?

Nancy hurried across the lawn to the modern building housing the practice rooms. It's amazing how few people are around on a Sunday, she thought. The Great Lawn was nearly deserted, with just a few sunbathers lying on deck chairs or blankets, soaking up the sun. As she crossed the lawn, several conversations played themselves out in her head. She heard Lucas saying, "I feel that his playing lacks heart." She heard Maura saying how pleased Ted would be at the change in judges.

The building itself was dark and cool. Since the practice rooms were on a lower level, no light filtered in from the outside. Nancy didn't know where the light switch was, so she had to feel her way down the staircase and through the dark maze of hallways.

She felt along the wall and finally found the master switch. All of the lights came on. The first room she decided to check was the room where she and Curt Lucas had talked the night before, the room with the sofa and chairs.

She opened the door and went straight to the piano. The piano seat had an embroidered cover. On a hunch Nancy lifted the cover and looked inside. Just as she thought, there was a lot of printed sheet music stored in it. As she searched through the papers, a tune ran through her head again and again. She started to hum it. Why was the tune so familiar? Was it just that she'd heard the band playing it the night before? Or was it something else?

After going through all the scores, she could see that Alfred Cole's score was not there. The tune played again in her head, and she stopped for a moment, concentrating on where she had heard it. Then all at once she remembered. It was the tune Ted had been humming as he held her in his arms when they danced.

Ted! It had to be him. With grim determination, Nancy decided to search all the practice rooms. Suddenly the lights went out and the room was plunged into darkness.

Nancy froze. She heard the door open and shut and paper rustling. A voice whispered, "If you're looking for this, it's too late." Then Nancy felt strong hands around her throat. She started to kick and scream, using all of her strength to throw off her assailant, but she could feel herself weakening.

Nancy was on the point of blacking out

when the room was suddenly flooded with light and the door was thrown open. Nancy freed herself and stepped back, gasping. Curt Lucas and Bess were standing there, and Nancy could finally face her attacker. It was Ted Martinelli.

# Chapter Sixteen

NANCY AND BESS SAT on the veranda of the Dandelion Inn, sipping iced tea from tall, cool glasses, enjoying the last rays of the late-afternoon sun. "I'll never forget seeing Ted's face," Nancy said to Bess, shuddering. "When I went to the police station after his arrest he was like a complete stranger. I felt as if I'd never known him at all. Tell me one thing, Bess," she added, "how did you guys find me?"

"Well, I got worried, and I decided to look for you," Bess began. "I ran into a very worried-looking Lucas on the lawn, and he said that he'd seen Ted following you. Lucas was investigating, and I insisted on coming, too.

"We were right behind Ted," Bess went on, "when he disappeared into the practice building. We followed him downstairs. When Ted flipped the light switch and everything went dark, we knew immediately that something was wrong. But neither of us expected to find Ted with his hands around your throat." Bess paused. "Oh, Nancy!" she continued quickly. "I'm so glad you're all right. But now it's your turn to tell me what you know. You're the one who heard his confession. And I want to know everything."

"Okay, I'll tell you what I know," Nancy said. "To begin with, Ted was blackmailing Lucas because he felt he didn't stand a chance of winning with Lucas judging the competition. He knew Lucas didn't think much of his playing. When he set out to search Lucas's rooms, he didn't know what he might find. He was looking for anything incriminating."

"How did he know there would be anything at all?" Bess asked. "Lucas has a good reputation, right?"

"Yes, but Ted's teacher was jealous of Lucas. She hinted to anyone who would listen that Lucas couldn't have written his early musicals without help from someone. Ted picked up on this, and after his bad encounter with Lucas at that competition a few years ago, he was ready to find whatever he could to make trouble for him." Nancy paused and added a sprig of mint to her iced tea.

"Anyway," she continued, "when Ted found Cole's score, he immediately realized what it was and decided to use it. He had no influence on who would replace Lucas, but anyone would have been better, from his point of view. The fact that it turned out to be a friend of his teacher's was just good luck."

"So why did he start hurting the other finalists?" Bess asked, confused.

"That was the way Ted operated," Nancy said, sighing. "He was so ambitious that he felt he had to do everything to ensure his winning first prize. He knew that if either of the other two finalists was put out of commission, a semifinalist would replace them. But he must have figured that the semifinalists would never be as good as the finalists had been, and he'd have a better chance against them.

"Anyway, he sabotaged Keiko's horse, hoping that her wrist would be badly damaged, and then he poisoned Alexander by chopping up a poisonous mushroom and putting it in his lunch box."

"How did he get that cut on his head?" Bess asked suddenly. "Did he do that to himself?"

Nancy nodded grimly. "Yes, he did. He used Maura's metronome from the common room to throw suspicion on her, and then he messed up his room himself, hoping to divert suspicion away from himself. And by the way, he was also the one responsible for the food poisoning in England last summer."

"You mean Maura?" Bess asked, amazed. "Why did he do that?"

"Apparently, he's had a grudge against Maura for a long time. In recent years, she seemed his most direct competition. They covered the same territory, always choosing the same music to play. He wanted her out of the way. In the end, it always came down to one thing," Nancy said sadly. "Ambition. Ambition got the better of him."

"What about the hazard sign on the road? How did he manage to get it there on his motorbike?"

"He borrowed Maura's car earlier in the day. He must have found the sign and put it behind a tree then, planning to return later and set it up," Nancy said. "He also put some sort of knockout drug in my drink and left it on the table when he brought our drinks, hoping that I'd pick it up."

"Why did he go after you like that?" Bess asked. "I don't understand."

"When he heard I was a detective, and Keiko asked me to investigate, he had no choice but to go along with it," Nancy said. "But he must have panicked. That's when

I think the idea first occurred to him to do everything he could to get in my way." She paused, scanning at the mountains just barely visible on the horizon. "In the end, he was angry enough to kill me. He almost succeeded."

Bess reached across the table and squeezed her friend's hand. "Oh, Nan! This has been so terrible for you."

Nancy smiled slightly and shook her head. She said, "It's good for me to talk it all out like this. Ted's room was the last one I searched in the dorm. Apparently, he had been in his room when he heard me climbing in through the window. He didn't know I was searching everyone's room. He decided I was onto him, and that terrified him. He sneaked out before I got inside, and then followed me afterward when I went to the practice building."

Bess's eyes grew wide. "He could have hurt you. If Curt hadn't been following him . . ."

"I know," Nancy said before Bess finished the thought. "But it's all over now. We've got lots to do, such as calling my father—"

"And give Mrs. W. her present," Bess added.

"And attend the piano competition finals," Nancy said. "Oh, yes, and relax," she finished with a laugh. "That is what we came for, isn't it?"

* * *

The next day was Monday, the day of the piano competition. Since Ted's arrest, Maura MacDonald had been elevated to the position of finalist. When Nancy and Bess saw her in the common room just before her concerto performance, she was relaxed and glowing.

"I'm sorry it had to happen like this, but I feel ready," Maura said. Nancy and Bess wished her good luck. As Maura left the room, Keiko arrived, clutching her concerto score.

"I have never been so nervous before a performance," she admitted shakily.

"Calm down," Nancy said, "you know this music inside out. You told us so yourself." Keiko nodded her agreement and sat down beside them on the sofa.

"Did you hear about Grace Hammel?" Keiko asked.

"No, what happened?" Nancy asked excitedly.

"She's been asked to step down because of what you overheard her saying at the club Saturday night."

After thinking about it all day Sunday, Nancy had finally decided to go to the head of the festival and describe what she had heard. When questioned in front of the committee at an emergency meeting, Grace had broken down and admitted that she planned to push for Alexander if he would do certain things for her in return, such as perform and teach part-time at her school. As a prizewinning Russian pianist, he would have brought her much-needed publicity, money, and new students. However, she said that Alexander had not wanted any part of it.

"I'm glad she's not judging," Nancy said. "People like that shouldn't be allowed to run schools or judge contests. Good for Alexander for not giving in."

"The judge replacing Grace is a well-known local pianist, and they were lucky to get her," Keiko said.

It was time for the finals, and Keiko left them in a nervous flurry. Nancy and Bess walked over to the auditorium where the piano concertos would be performed. They were joined by Curt Lucas.

He smiled warmly at both of them, then said to Nancy, "First thing this morning I called ASCAP, the American composers' society, and told them the whole story about Alfred's themes. They want me to come down and explain to the committee next week."

"How do you feel about it?" Nancy asked.

"Very relieved, I think," Lucas said. "Alfred should always have gotten credit for those themes, and now he will."

"I'm happy for you," Nancy said. As they walked into the crowded auditorium and took their seats, the lights dimmed, and there was an expectant hush. The chairperson of the piano competition walked to the center of the stage and said into the microphone, "Ladies and gentlemen, you are about to hear performances by three of the most promising young pianists of their generation."

Keiko, Bess, and Nancy sat on the Great Lawn under a shady tree. Keiko was waiting to hear the judges' decision, which was to be announced in a few moments.

A woman in a yellow dress started walking across the lawn in their direction, holding a piece of paper. Keiko watched her nervously. When the woman had almost reached them, she waved the piece of paper and grinned. Nancy looked at Keiko and smiled.

"It looks like this contest is all yours, Keiko," she said.

## Nancy's next case:

The Great Lakes High School Press Association is convening at the River Heights Atrium Hotel, a luxury palace of marble and glass. But for Nancy it's turning into a house of sabotage and suspicion. Someone has targeted the beautiful, Italian-born student Gina Fiorella for harm . . . and she's targeted Ned Nickerson for romance!

Gina's father is a man of immense wealth and political power, and she may be the victim of one of his numerous enemies. But the more Nancy investigates, the deeper the mystery becomes. Hidden behind the hotel's magnificent facade lurks a tangle of secret ambitions—sinister desires that could prove fatal. Not only for Gina, but to Nancy as well . . . in *Hidden Meanings,* Case #110 in The Nancy Drew Files®.